A CAPITAL CRIME

KATE P ADAMS

Copyright © Kate P Adams 2021

The right of Kate P Adams to be identified as the author of this work has been asserted by her in accordance with the Copyright, Designs and Patents Act 1988.

All rights reserved. No part of this publication may be reproduced, transmitted, or stored in a retrieval system, in any form or by any means, without permission in writing from the author, nor be otherwise circulated in any form of binding or cover other than that in which it is published and without similar condition being imposed on the subsequent purchaser.

All characters in this publication, other than those clearly in the public domain, are fictitious and any resemblance to real people, alive or dead, is purely coincidental.

Paperback ISBN

Cover design by Dar Albert

ALSO BY KATE P ADAMS

Death by Dark Roast
A Killer Wedding
Sleep Like the Dead
A Deadly Ride
Mulled Wine and Murder
A Tragic Act
A Capital Crime

*For my friend,
Rosanna Summers*

CHAPTER 1

The packet of shortbread biscuits was empty, and we were now making our way through the sticky buns as the train raced through suburb after suburb on its way to London. We were less than half an hour into a two-hour journey, but as we passed through Derby, we'd been unable to resist breaking into the snacks. It was eight o'clock in the morning, so the cans of gin and tonic and little bottles of prosecco remained unopened. We were draining bucket-sized cups of coffee as we relaxed into our seats and I worried slightly about my inability to get another decent shot of caffeine until we arrived at St Pancras.

'I hope we get plenty of time to go out and play,' said Joyce as she flicked through a guidebook to the best cocktail bars in London. 'I've been marking off those I want to go to, and I'll be dragging you two along. First stop is Dukes where Ian Fleming got the idea for James Bond's *shaken, not stirred*. It's around the corner from the house, so I believe that will be our first stop.'

'I hate to break it to you,' said Mark lazily without looking up from his book, 'but James Bond is fictional. You are not going to run into him at Dukes, so you are not going to be Joyce Bond any time soon.' I couldn't help but picture her in a figure-hugging black dress, martini in hand and introducing herself as *Bond, Joyce Bond*.

'No, but I might run into an eligible viscount who doesn't have a habit of dashing off overseas at a moment's notice and bedding any nubile young woman he claps eyes on.'

'Don't get your hopes up, most of those bars will be propped up by tourists these days.'

'Wealthy, handsome tourists, in all likelihood. Don't try and pour cold water over my plans, Mark Boxer. You'll be laughing on the other side of that moustache when I wave you both off in a couple of weeks' time: you returning north, I moving into a palatial villa on the banks of the Thames to start my life with Baron Stinking Rich.'

I enjoyed my friends bantering, although I felt a touch of sadness as I listened to Joyce. In reality, she had no interest in a man's bank balance; not that one dripping with cash would be a bad thing. She was still searching for Mr Right, and being of indeterminate – although rather mature – years was not getting in her way. That immediately cheered me up; her determination and optimism were things we singletons could all take a lesson from.

I stared out of the window, nibbling on another sticky bun which had mysteriously found its way into my hand and watching the green meadows and the farms as they shot past, the tractors rumbling from one field to another. As we neared towns, we'd roll through industrial estates and along the ends of people's gardens. I hadn't returned to London since I'd started working at Charleton House two years ago. No particular reason, life had simply run away with me, although I did feel a little bad for not making more of an effort to visit the friends I had left behind. The ex-fiancé, not so much. This current trip was, in theory, business not pleasure, but I had no doubt that we'd make it a time to remember.

My employers, the Duke and Duchess of Ravensbury, were

taking some of their most well-known and interesting pieces of art from Charleton House, their dazzling stately home in Derbyshire, and displaying them at their London home, Ravensbury House. The exhibition was temporary and would last only for the summer, but the hope was it would encourage more people to travel to Derbyshire and visit the vast house and its 40,000-acre estate in person. As the Head of Catering, I had been asked to design a menu for a pop-up café and go to London to ensure the food and service matched the standards of those we insisted on back at Charleton House, as well as oversee the training of the new staff. Joyce Brocklehurst, Head of Retail, was doing the same for a small shop, and Mark would be delivering guided tours to the VIP guests who would attend the special events being held in the first week. After that, we would all travel home.

'Oi, leave some for us.' Joyce slapped the back of Mark's hand as it moved from crisp packet to mouth without him raising his eyes from the page he was studying intently. 'Is it too early to open this?' She was spinning a small bottle of prosecco round and round in her hands.

'Well, if you keep doing that, all you're going to achieve is spraying it over us,' I told her as I took it from her and set it on the table, 'and I'm sure it's a dreadful addition to coffee, so yes, it is too early.'

She huffed like a fed-up child, and then pulled a copy of *Vogue* out of her bag and settled down.

'So you've finally decided to take some style advice from the experts?' Mark asked with amusement in his voice.

'Don't rise to it, Joyce,' I advised. 'I for one am grateful you've worn such a bright orange coat; at least this way, I won't lose you in the crowds.'

'And hopefully all the wasps will head your way and avoid my lunch,' added Mark. The long orange trench coat Joyce had opted to wear was, in my opinion, the perfect summer choice. I wasn't so sure about the lime-green t-shirt she wore underneath, but Mark did have a point and I hated wasps.

With the pair of them finally quiet, I thought about our glorious, gritty and romantic capital city, feeling the familiar swell of excitement that I had experienced intermittently over the last week. I had a love-hate relationship with London. My love of history was well and truly fed in the city and was looking forward to being sated again; I was fascinated by the beautiful architecture and enjoyed wandering in London's parks, and I had a long list of museums I wanted to revisit. As well as all that, I was sure I would waste a great deal of time simply enjoying the calming effects of sitting near the Thames and watching the world go by. I hadn't realised until this moment how keen I was to return.

WE ROLLED into St Pancras station. A masterpiece of Victorian Gothic architecture, it had been thoroughly spruced up some years ago when it had become the London station for the Eurostar, its restoration revealing a thing of beauty. Mark lifted my bag down off the luggage rack – at barely five feet tall, I could never get a bag up to or down from there unaided – and then helped Joyce.

'What the hell is in this?' puffed Mark as he retrieved her suitcase. 'You got a body in it?'

'Not yet, but I'm planning on putting yours in it once you start irritating me, which will probably be by the end of the day.'

I wondered if I was experiencing what parents felt when they took their bickering children away on holiday. I was almost entirely grey-haired already, and this trip was showing signs of finishing off the job, maybe even sending my hair completely white.

I steered Joyce away from the champagne bar and Mark away from the bookshop, and led the way out to the taxi rank. The July sunshine welcomed us, along with the sounds of the busy Euston Road. We clambered into a black cab and, after giving the driver the address, I settled back into the seat. There was something about being in an iconic black cab that made me feel like a grown up. That was ridiculous, of course, but when I was a child it had always seemed like something that only people on TV did.

Joyce and Mark stared out of the window, watching the city go by, and I did the same, enjoying the sense of familiarity as we drove through Russell Square and glimpsed the British Museum. Tourists packed the pavements of Shaftesbury Avenue and spilled out onto the road at Piccadilly Circus. Eventually, we turned onto Pall Mall – named after a croquet-like ball game – travelling past the gentlemen's clubs in grand lofty buildings with their Doric and Corinthian columns. Finally, we slipped along a narrow street which eventually widened out, presenting us with the view of a sumptuous 18th-century Palladian mansion. It was strange to think of this as a 'second home', a city getaway. But that's exactly what it was to the Fitzwilliam-Scott family. Being a Duke and Duchess really did come with its perks.

CHAPTER 2

I watched as Joyce lifted her suitcase out of the cab with none of the exertion that Mark had displayed.

'Not bad,' Mark declared as he stood in the middle of the road, taking the house in. 'I'm disappointed there's no red carpet or guard of honour to welcome us, but give me time and I'm sure I can forgive.'

'Come on!' called Joyce as she dragged the lurid pink suitcase towards the entrance, tugging it over the kerb. 'You're not being paid to stand outside gawping.'

The entrance hall was an elegantly decorated, dignified room. Ornamental plaster ran around the edge of the ceiling and a row of busts was lined up opposite a large fireplace. I was surprised; I'd expected a wildly opulent room.

'Ah, Sophie, and Mark, Joyce too, welcome, welcome.' Alexander Fitzwilliam-Scott, the 12th Duke of Ravensbury, Viscount Earlfield, Baron Hadbury, spread his arms wide. 'Your first visit to Ravensbury House, I believe. Well, come on in. Leave your suitcases in here, they'll be perfectly safe.' The Duke was a thin man, handsome with a patrician nose that paired well with his aristocratic bearing. His shirtsleeves were rolled up, revealing the tanned arms that were evidence of his recent trip to the South of France with the Duchess. 'We're not quite ready, but we will be, we will be. The final hangings are taking place today, and then we'll give everything a once-over tomorrow.' He carried on talking as he led us from room to room, so I had no time to take anything in properly; it was a blur of chandeliers, richly decorated carpets and gold leaf shimmering everywhere. Clearly, the understated entrance hall was not a good example of things to come as we scurried from the dining room to the music room.

The Duke's enthusiasm for the exhibition was clear. 'Joyce, everything has arrived for the shop, and I believe it's being laid out to your instructions. At least, I hope for the team's sake it is.' He gave a little smile; he knew Joyce's fierce reputation as well as anybody. 'Sophie, for the café, everything has arrived except the furniture. Fairly fundamental, I appreciate that, but I believe it's on its way. I'll leave you to chase that up. Mark—' He stopped and turned to face us. 'Mark, I imagine you already know more about this place than I do. Well, what do you think? Not bad, eh? I don't spend as much time here as I'd like, but I am very fond of the place. Well, tour over, must get on. Very glad you're all here.' He gave Mark a manly pat on the arm as he strode out.

'Careful, Mark,' I advised. 'I think you've got a strong competitor there for the role of tour guide extraordinaire.'

'Never mind the tours, where's my bloody shop? I need to see what mess has been made of it.' Joyce marched out. It was time for her team to meet their new boss and I quietly wished them luck. I was a little more laid back. I'd been keeping an eye on things from Derbyshire, and I'd already known the furniture was late, but I'd been promised it would be delivered in the morning. I was familiar with the agency providing my café staff and trusted their decisions. Much of the food was being sourced from our usual Derbyshire-based suppliers in order to ensure a full Charleton experience. I also felt on firm ground simply because I had lived and worked in London for over ten years. I might never have been in Ravensbury House before, but it felt a little like coming home.

MY LITTLE CAFÉ was located in what had been a large study. I smiled to myself as I took in the rows of mahogany shelves, the books tucked away behind glass doors and the comfortable leather chairs at one end of the room. It felt like a close cousin to the Library Café, my favourite of the three I managed back at Charleton House; I was definitely on familiar territory.

A large part of the room was empty, waiting for the tables and chairs that would arrive in the morning. The windows to one side had a rather dull view out to a neighbouring building and didn't provide a lot of light, but the beautiful room more than made up for that. One door led to a flight of stairs which descended to a basement kitchen, and another to a small enclosed courtyard. Flower boxes lined the edges, and against one wall, a hydrangea climbed a large trellis towards the blue sky above. This was a delightful little corner and I was grateful to have an outdoor area attached to the café, no matter how small.

Joyce's shop, on the other hand, was a sunny room painted in a delicate cream colour. This had been the morning room, where guests to the house would wait while their host was fetched. Antique tables had an array of attractive items displayed upon them, books about the Fitzwilliam-Scott family side by side with those on the history of art. Charleton House-branded chocolates, jam, and coffee looked extremely enticing. Postcards had been made that focused on the art brought down to London, and others showed attractive photographs of Ravensbury House itself. Joyce was barking orders at two timid-looking girls, but she did at least intersperse her barks with compliments when things were as she wanted them.

. . .

A COUPLE OF HOURS LATER, Mark stood in the doorway that divided the two rooms. 'How goes it, girls? Is everything to your liking, Ms Brocklehurst? I know that you have very exacting standards.'

'Are you at a loose end, by any chance? Because if so, you can unpack those mugs, and if you break one, I'll make sure it's taken out of your wages.'

Her assistants looked at one another, wide-eyed.

'Don't worry,' I reassured them. 'Mark is a special case.'

'Very *special*,' Joyce confirmed.

'I'm extremely busy! I spent some time with the Duke, talking about some of the notable guests they've had here over the years. A number of prime ministers have popped round – William Pitt and William Gladstone both lived in St James's and would come over. Nancy Astor, the first woman to sit in Parliament, liked a good party, threw some corkers. You'd have liked her, Joyce, she and Churchill had some fabulous exchanges. He told her that having a woman in Parliament was like having one intrude on him in the bathroom, and she told him, *"You're not handsome enough to have such fears".* We both laughed out loud and I saw Joyce fighting the urge to smile. 'When she said to him, *"If you were my husband, I'd poison your tea",* he replied with, *"Madam, if you were my wife, I'd drink it!"'* At that, Joyce spluttered out a laugh.

'Alright, very amusing, but I do need to get on. Go on, shoo, both of you.'

I followed Mark out into the entrance hall where we ran into a young woman coming down the stairs.

'Sophie, great, you're here. I wanted to give you a heads up. The Duke and Duchess are both going to be having guests this evening, but it doesn't affect anything. If you'd planned on working late, you can carry on as usual; they know things won't be tidy down here.' Molly Flinders was the London-based assistant for the Duke and Duchess. Their lives in Derbyshire were so busy and their responsibilities so wide-ranging that their usual assistant couldn't be spared. Instead, Molly lived in London and managed Ravensbury House and their London affairs in their absence. I had met her a few times when she had visited Derbyshire. Her disconcertingly youthful looks belied her true age: she was in her early thirties and incredibly – some might say annoyingly – efficient. Although protective of the Duke and Duchess's diary, she guarded it with a smile and a gentleness that made everyone want to please her and agree to whatever she suggested. I liked her a lot – we'd had some memorable evenings together in the Black Swan pub.

'Can I do anything to help?' I asked.

'No, the Duchess is making a light meal upstairs for a friend, and the Duke's party will be coming back from a restaurant so they'll just be having drinks. They'll mainly be in the exhibition spaces.'

'A sneak peek!'

'Sort of; it's Dr Ambrose Pitkin, who will be giving a talk at Friday night's reception about the botanic illustrations, Dr Caleb Orne, the Head of the Botany Department at the Natural History Museum, and Gideon Snable-Bowers, the Earl of Baxworth and a friend of the Duke who is also a botanist. You might be interested in the Duchess's guest, Fleur Lazarus. She's remarkable, she's climbed Everest twice and recently came back from K2. She's giving a series of talks at the Royal Geographical Society next week and I'm hoping to go to one.'

'Ah, Molly, there you are.' The Duke had appeared in a doorway. 'Two of the conservation team are late for their train, could you possibly drive them up to Euston Station? We know it will take you no time at all to get there.' Molly agreed and the Duke's amused smile risked breaking into laughter as he walked away.

'What was that all about?' I asked. Molly looked a little embarrassed.

'I was caught on a speeding camera a couple of weeks ago. I was in Oliver's car.' I knew she was referring to Lord Oliver, the youngest of the three Fitzwilliam-Scott children. 'He often leaves it here and I'm allowed to borrow it from time to time. The Duke was very sweet afterwards, but he does keep teasing me about it, and in front of others. I consider it my punishment. I should go if they're not to miss their train, especially as I plan on driving like my ninety-year-old grandmother from now on. I'll be working late tonight if you need me for anything.' She smiled at us before dashing up the stairs two at a time.

'I like the way she didn't think I'd be working late and need to know,' Mark said, pretending to be put out.

'I'm saying nothing.'

'Very wise. Do you fancy going for a drink later? There's somewhere I want to take you and, if she behaves, Joyce too; it's on her list of must-see bars.'

'One minute you're complaining that someone might think you don't work very hard, and in the next breath, you're talking about going for a drink. Alright. It might be quite late, but sure.'

'It's a date. I'm off to rehearse the Palm Room part of my tour; I know I'll get a lot of questions about that.' He was bouncing gently from foot to foot as he moved off, keen to get started. He'd spent the last couple of weeks regaling me with stories of Ravensbury House, but having never been, I wasn't overly interested as they didn't mean a great deal to me. Besides, I was distracted getting everything I needed ready and making sure I had done all I could to prepare my teams back at Charleton House before I left them. It was easier to understand his enthusiasm now I was here; it was like a pocket-sized Charleton House. Gloriously opulent, but much more manageable, it wasn't large enough to be overwhelming. I knew I was going to enjoy my time here.

CHAPTER 3

Dr Ambrose Pitkin stood in front of a collection of highly detailed, richly coloured paintings of exotic plants, butterflies, birds, and even some insects. He quietly took them all in, tapping a finger on his chin, running his eyes from one picture to another.

'Perfect, just perfect,' he declared. 'The light in here will be spectacular during the day; I swear I can see the wings move, and at any point they are going to be flapping around our heads. And the colours – I feel they were painted only yesterday.' He sighed, grasping the Duke by the hand and shaking it firmly. 'She never sought the limelight, hated all this…' he waved his arms around the room '…formality and fuss. Much rather be out in the jungle. But I think she would have approved.'

Dr Pitkin wasn't particularly tall, with a rounded middle, half-moon specs and leather patches on the elbows of his blazer. If I hadn't recognised his name, I would have easily guessed he was a scientist.

His eyes shone through his spectacles. 'Did you inherit any of her artistic talent yourself?' he asked the Duke, who laughed in response.

'Not a jot. My wife possesses that particular leaning, but no, I'm afraid Caroline's talents did not make it down to me.'

'Well, you're doing your bit, sharing these with the world.' This time it was Dr Caleb Orne who spoke. 'It's extremely generous of you to donate them to the Natural History Museum.'

When the Duke had returned from the restaurant with his friends, he had seen the light on in the café and popped his head around the door, inviting me to look at the paintings with the 'experts'. The paintings were wonderful, but I was getting increasingly confused by the conversation.

'I'm sorry, Sophie, we did rather dive in.' The Duke had clearly noticed my baffled expression. 'These paintings are the work of Caroline Annabelle Fitzwilliam-Scott. Her brother was the 9th Duke, my great-grandfather. He was artistic, too, loved literature – their father was a friend of Charles Dickens – but I've yet to find evidence he ever left the country. His sister, on the other hand,' he indicated the paintings with a wave of his hand, 'remarkable woman, rarely at home. Her interests combined both art and science. Ambrose knows more about her than I do.'

'I don't know about that, but I have spent quite a lot of time studying her work. I can tell you she wasn't the most patient of people. She was quite a loner, hated parties, and considered a good cup of tea much more favourable to marriage. Caroline was truly happy in the forests of Brazil, the outback of Australia. She packed light, only ever taking one small suitcase with her and a case of painting supplies. Her suitcase is over there.' I looked over at a small, battered leather suitcase which looked as if it would fall apart at any moment, and found myself wondering about all the amazing places it had been. 'Now, this is a wonderful example of her work, the Hypothyris Ninonia Scotti. Caroline discovered a number of new species of butterfly and this was one of them. It's a glass-wing butterfly, not the most gaudy, but very pretty, I'm sure you'll agree. She also made a significant contribution to our understanding of flora and fauna in certain parts of the world. She was utterly driven and singular in her interests. It has to be said that she paid little attention to the people and politics of the places she visited, but her focus has resulted in some fabulous discoveries and these exceptional records of the natural world.'

'Not that Gideon agrees, eh?' added the Duke.

Despite the small audience, Dr Ambrose Pitkin had given an energetic performance. He was the ideal person to communicate Caroline's remarkable achievements, but it had been impossible for me not to notice that Gideon Snable-Bowers, the Earl of Baxworth, had looked less than impressed. I wasn't sure if he was amused or if it was a sneer that I saw on his face.

'Oh, you know how I feel, Alex. I don't agree entirely with Ambrose's assessment; Caroline deserves a great deal of credit, just not all of it. But you also know I'm not inclined to make a fuss.' He smiled, but I still couldn't interpret the sentiment behind it.

'Glad to hear it. Now then, I have a rather magnificent thirty-year-old single malt waiting for us. Care to join me, gentlemen? Sophie, you really ought to be going home, it's… eight o'clock.'

'Don't worry, Your Grace, I'm here to call an end to her day.' Mark stepped into the room and stood beside me. It was unusual to hear him use the correct term when addressing the Duke – we'd been instructed to use 'Duke' or 'Duchess', except on formal occasions or around other guests.

'Very pleased to hear it, Mark. Goodnight.'

We excused ourselves and left the four men to their evening. I was disappointed not to have met Fleur Lazarus, only having heard her voice as she arrived earlier, but perhaps I could attend her talk with Molly next week. Right now, all I could think about was a drink to round off a very long day.

. . .

'WE CAN COME BACK for our bags. Come on, I've reserved us a table. It's only round the corner.'

Joyce had already returned to the serviced apartment that she and Mark were staying in, so it was just the two of us. The bounce still very firmly in his step, Mark launched himself out onto the street. He wasn't kidding; in less than a minute, we were standing outside a hotel with 'DUKES' above the door on a bright blue sign. He grinned and led the way. We were seated in the bar by a smartly dressed man in a white jacket.

'Two martinis, please,' Mark ordered immediately.

'Am I not allowed to choose my own drink?' I asked, trying to sound put out.

'You don't want anything else at Dukes. This is the home of the martini. It was Ian Fleming's hang-out, and it's here, legend has it, that he coined the phrase *shaken, not stirred.*'

'Yes, I know. Joyce told us that earlier, remember?'

Mark carried on as if I hadn't spoken. 'I will *not* allow you to have any old gin and tonic.'

We were sitting in comfortable deep-blue velvet armchairs in a small room with a wooden bar at one end. It was already quite busy and there wasn't a pair of jeans or trainers in sight. Mark looked very much at home in his trademark waistcoat. Today's was a smart navy blue affair with fine pink stripes and a bright pink silk back, and with his well-groomed moustache and pocket watch on its gold chain, he was the picture of elegance.

A waiter returned to our table with a trolley, two frozen glasses and a bottle of London Dry gin that had clearly been in the freezer; there wasn't an ice cube in sight. With that, some dry vermouth and lemon zest, he made what looked like an incredibly strong drink. There was no shaking and no stirring.

'Chin-chin,' said Mark as he brought the glass to his lips, 'here's to our week in London.' The drink was strong, but it was also smooth, and the citrus was wonderfully refreshing. As the liquid warmed in my mouth, I started to taste the botanicals in the gin. It was delicious. I took another look at the room; it was easy to imagine James Bond leaning rakishly at the bar and surveying his surroundings with an air of confidence.

'Are you all set, or do you still have a lot to do to get ready before the reception on Thursday?' Mark asked. 'There is going to be a lot of blue blood in attendance with some very high standards – not that you can't meet and exceed those standards, of course.'

'I'm not catering it, thank goodness, and the café doesn't go into operation until we open to the public on the weekend, so I have plenty of time to iron out any kinks.'

'Ooh, a kinky café, I like the sound of that.' I rolled my eyes at him and considered how my quota of ocular rotations had gone up considerably since I'd met Mark.

'Anyone in particular I should look out for at the reception?'

'Yes, actually, you've not met Oliver yet, have you?' Lord Oliver was, for all intents and purposes, the black sheep of the Fitzwilliam-Scott family. From what I knew of him, he preferred partying in London nightclubs to paying a visit to the family seat in Derbyshire, which I assumed he considered a rather parochial backwater. He was totally unlike his two older siblings who had established successful careers and appeared to lead settled and respectable lives. His brother Edward was an architect living in New York, so he wouldn't be attending the reception, but the eldest of the three, Annabelle, would no doubt be in attendance.

'No. Is he still at university? What does he do?' I had never been very clear on how he supported himself, if that was what he did.'

'Pester his parents for money, mainly. He started but never finished a postgraduate degree – an excuse to avoid finding a job, if you ask me – then he was in hedge fund management for a while. Whatever that is, I've never understood it. Then he was involved with a record company, and now he's in property management. How successful he is, I don't know, but he's always popping up in photos of exclusive parties and on private yachts.'

I could tell from his tone that Mark wasn't keen on the man. 'What's he like to talk to?'

'I do my best not to, is the easiest way to answer that. Speak of the devil!' Mark was facing a window. 'I didn't see him in here; he must have been in the restaurant or out in the cigar garden.'

I turned just in time to see a blond-haired man walk past the window before stopping and calling over his shoulder. He laughed at something, and then kept on walking as a taller man with a fuller figure in a linen suit caught up with him. They moved out of sight and I found myself holding my breath, staring at the now empty street.

It couldn't be, although I had known there was a chance I would run into him while I was here. Despite London being an enormous city with a population of nine million, it is remarkably easy to encounter people you know there.

I forced myself to breathe and took a long draught of my martini. This time, a sip just wouldn't cut it.

'Take it easy, we're not in any rush.' Mark laughed as he watched me knock back a great gulp of liquid. It couldn't have been him, could it? My ex fiancé, Adam Campbell, in the company of Lord Oliver Fitzwilliam-Scott? It was too great a coincidence, and yet I was so certain of what I had seen.

There was a strong chance this wouldn't be my last martini of the night.

CHAPTER 4

I woke with light streaming in through my bedroom window and stretched, forgetting that I was lying on a futon in a room barely bigger than the mattress and promptly punching the wall. I pulled myself up into a sitting position and found myself being stared at intently by a furball next to the half-open door.

I put my glasses on. The furball was a rather beautiful light gingery-brown Persian cat. Penny the Persian, to be precise. Her flat face, prominent eyebrows and permanent scowl gave her an appearance of deep irritation, but I knew her to be the sweetest little thing. She was the owner of Zannah Rowe, a close friend who had been quick to offer me the use of her spare room when she heard I would be back in the city. The Duke and Duchess had offered to provide accommodation for everyone who had travelled down from Derbyshire, but I much preferred the opportunity to spend time with Zannah.

'Sorry,' a voice called. 'Did she wake you?' Zannah's arm appeared around the door, holding a large coffee mug.

'I'm decent, you can come in.'

She stepped over Penny and sat on the end of the bed. 'Sleep okay?'

'Mmmm,' I replied as I took my first sip of coffee.

'I hope it matches your painfully high standards. I'm guessing you're as much of a coffee snob as ever.'

'I am, and it passes the test. Do I get it delivered to my bed every morning?'

'Absolutely, and your kippers will be delivered on a silver platter in a few moments, madam,' she said with a familiar bounce in her voice, giving my foot a squeeze and settling back against the wall.

Zannah had been my best friend when I lived in London. She worked at the Natural History Museum and I'd spent many a happy hour in exhibitions there courtesy of the free tickets she gave me. We'd spent most of last night apologising to one another for not making more of an effort to keep in touch; I'd stayed countless nights in this room after wild evenings out where the alcohol had flowed a little too easily, or girls' nights in with films and ice cream. When my relationship had crashed and burned, this was where I had holed up until I had felt strong enough to return to the flat I had shared with Adam in order to collect my belongings. The room wasn't big enough to swing a Persian cat and the futon was at floor level, which was no longer quite as easy as I remembered to get up from, but it was cosy and her flat was a second home to me.

'So, have you slept on it?' she asked, raising a perky eyebrow. 'Was it him?'

'Oh, I don't know.' I sighed. 'I was so sure it was. It looked like him, and I *felt* it was him, but that might just have been because I've spent so much time wondering if I'll run into him.'

'And you didn't get a good look at him.'

'True, but there's still a nagging part of me that thinks I'm right.'

Penny wandered over and settled down next to me.

'What would Adam be doing with... what was his name? Oliver?'

'Uh-huh, Lord Oliver Fitzwilliam-Scott.'

'Blimey, Adam has gone up in the world. Prison one minute, then friends with the aristocracy the next.'

'That's the bit that makes me doubt the whole thing. How that could happen, I have no idea, and it's a bit of a coincidence that my ex-fiancé is friends with the son of my employer.'

Zannah grinned. 'See, you've nothing to worry about, it was nothing more than the effect of a very strong martini. So you can relax, enjoy my hospitality and run amok in the Big Smoke. Top-up?'

I nodded. As she left to get more coffee, I leaned back against the wall and closed my eyes. It was *so* nice to be back with Zannah. As well as being a good friend, she was like a human happy pill. She was enthusiastic about any and everything; she could be asking the time of day and it would come out with a breathy enthusiasm that made it sound like it was the most vital information she had ever sought. And the gratitude that followed your answer would be equally effusive. Her bottle-blonde elfin haircut and piercing blue eyes added to the bubbly impression. I was sure that some people found her exhausting, but I found her energy contagious, and she saved me the expense and illegality of taking drugs.

AFTER A QUICK BREAKFAST, Zannah waved me off with a travel mug of coffee. She cycled to the museum each day and set off ringing her bell. She lived about ten minutes' drive south of the River Thames in a suburb called Earlsfield, only a short walk from Wimbledon's famous All England Lawn Tennis Club where we'd been fortunate enough to get a number of tickets over the years and enjoyed many a glass of champagne with strawberries and cream. Today, however, I was hotfooting it to the station to start my commute to Ravensbury House.

I hadn't done what you could really call a commute since leaving London, but it was made easier by being quite short by London standards at only forty minutes. A packed train ride spent staring into someone's armpit, followed by a mad dash for the Tube, couldn't have been more different to my peaceful drive through the Charleton estate every morning. But, the sun was shining, the journey was a novelty, and the final walk along the edge of Green Park with its mature trees and grassland was enough to start my day with a spring in my step.

As I got closer to the house, my path was blocked by police tape where a large section of the park, and my route, had been cordoned off. A small white tent had been erected next to the base of a tree where a couple of people in white all-in-one suits were talking. A uniformed officer was patrolling the edge of the cordon and redirecting people. I didn't mind having to take a longer route around; after all, someone was clearly having a much worse day than me.

I ARRIVED as two of the marble busts on the plinths in the entrance hall were being replaced with modern bronze busts of the current Duke and Duchess of Ravensbury.

'Soph, your chairs are out back,' called Mark as he dashed past, carrying an armful of 'room folders' that visitors could read in order to learn more about the rooms, their history and contents. Mark had spent weeks putting them together, work made harder as the Duke and Duchess regularly changed their minds about which artwork they were going to bring down from Derbyshire for the exhibition.

'Do you need a hand?' I smiled as I heard the familiar voice and turned to face Chelsea Morris, a young café assistant who worked with me back at Charleton House. I had decided that it was time to give her more experience and had asked her to come and join me for the first week; I needed someone who knew how I liked to work and could help guide the other members of the team. She was young, but enthusiastic and incredibly capable. I gave her a big hug and took her suitcase from her.

'Come on, I'll show you around and make you a coffee. You must have been up at the crack of dawn?'

'It was quite early, but it was okay; I slept a lot of the way down.' She looked a little bashful at that admission.

'I wish I had. Instead, I had to listen to those two for most of the journey.' I nodded towards Mark as he was being thrown out of the shop to a shout of *'Get out, you're not wanted in here'* from Joyce.

After making us both a coffee I set to work with Chelsea, fetching the wooden furniture that had been stacked up outside, still covered in plastic, and placing it around the study. I hadn't been sure how the rather industrial-looking modern chairs and tables would look against the backdrop of the 18th-century study with all its dark wood, leather armchairs and heavily decorated ceiling plaster, but they actually worked rather well, a fitting reflection of the contemporary art mixed in amongst the classical pieces in the exhibition.

As we worked, Chelsea told me about the carers who would be helping with her father while she was away. He had multiple sclerosis and her mother was no longer around, leaving Chelsea to be his main carer. Balancing this with her job had led to some problems, and her performance at work had suffered, but once I'd learnt about her responsibilities outside of work, my team and I had done all we could to support her. She'd blossomed as a result and I was so proud of her. The local authority had arranged for additional care so she could take this opportunity, and her father had been keen for her to come.

'He's worried, though. I've never been to London before and...'

'Hang on,' I interrupted, 'never?' She shook her head. 'This is your first trip alone, and you found your way from St Pancras Station? I'd have met you if I'd known.'

'It was fine. I had to ask for directions a few times, but it's just like going into Sheffield, only busier.' That was an understatement, and I had even more appreciation for her determination to get on with things. This girl was sure to go far.

'Do you have any milk?' Molly had appeared at the door.

'Are you okay? You look a little pale. Can I get you something to drink?'

She shook her head. 'No thanks, it's just the shock.'

'What's happened?'

'I don't know if you've been through the park today, but a body was found early this morning. It was Ambrose, Dr Ambrose Pitkin.'

I put the carton of milk on the counter, but kept hold of it, unable to let go as the news sank in.

CHAPTER 5

'Bloody hell, Sophie, did you have to bring your death curse to London with you?'

Mark and I were sitting outside the front of the house, opting for a seat on the edge of the kerb in the sun. Once the news of Dr Pitkin's death had spread around the small number of staff, it felt as though everyone had started to sleepwalk through their work. Mark and I had been unable to find a key that would let us onto the terrace at the back of the house, and it didn't seem the time to ask anyone else where it was. So instead, we'd carried our cups of coffee out here and like a pair of street urchins, were perching at the side of the road, taking in the news.

'I guess you take a bit of a risk cutting through the park at night,' Mark mused. 'Maybe someone watched him leave here and assumed he had money.'

As we chatted, two men walked down the street and past us into the house. One of them, who looked as though he spent every spare hour in the gym and could face down an elephant charge, gave me a quizzical look. The other had a face that screamed 'get me more coffee' and just ignored us.

'Police,' said Mark.

'How do you know?'

'It's a sixth sense I have. That and a man has been killed on his way home from here less than twenty-four hours ago. His body was found round the corner, and the police have had enough time to make a few calls and find out where he was last night. They're in suits, but trying to look tough rather than suave and sophisticated, and they have mud on their shoes so I guess they came straight from the park. How am I doing? Do I deserve my own deerstalker yet?'

'Not bad, but if you could tell me who killed Dr Pitkin, I'd be more impressed.'

'Nah, I'll leave that to you.'

I heard Joyce's heels before I saw her. 'What in the devil's name are you doing down there? Sophie, dignity, please. No lady sits on the kerb of a street, unless she's touting for business. Up. Mark, you, on the other hand, belong down there.'

'*We are all in the gutter, but some of us are looking at the stars,*' he declared with a flourish, quoting Oscar Wilde.

'I don't even know what that means. Just get up, you fool.'

Mark stood, and then offered me his hand. I grabbed it and heaved myself up.

'We should find out if the police want to talk to us. After all, we saw him last night.'

Mark nodded.

'And after that, I'm going to suggest we all take the rest of the day off, send our teams home, too.' I turned to see if Joyce looked quite well. It wasn't like her to allow people to slack off. 'I seriously doubt anyone is going to do much work after this,' she explained. 'Everyone's going to be distracted, and what little work they do get done will likely be littered with mistakes.'

'So it's less a concern for people's feelings and more that you don't want them stuffing up their job and damaging your shop stock,' said Mark.

'One and the same, Mark. I thought you'd be pleasantly

surprised; I know you consider me to be Cruella de Vil's even more wicked older sister, but beneath this glamorous exterior, there does indeed lie a beating heart.'

'I've never doubted that for a minute,' he replied. 'But we might disagree on what it's made of.'

As I brushed myself off, I spotted a uniformed officer with a police dog. They appeared to have followed the route that Dr Pitkin was likely to have taken from the house to Green Park.

'Come on,' said Joyce, sounding impatient. 'Quite apart from anything else, that bin stinks.' A large industrial rubbish bin stood at the end of an alleyway with its lid hanging open; it had been emptied that morning, but the smell that lingered occasionally wafted over in the breeze. I hated seeing litter lying around, so I went to pick up a few bits of rubbish that had not made it into the lorry: a couple of empty crisp packets, a Coke can and something that sparkled next to the black wheels of the bin.

It was a knife, and I knew instinctively that I shouldn't pick it up.

Resisting the urge to get too close to the knife, I called over the police officer with the dog. He seemed very interested in it, interested enough to suggest the suited and booted detectives come back outside.

Detective Inspector Grey and Detective Sergeant Knapp were polite but very formal throughout the interview that followed, the muscle-bound sergeant playing good cop to his boss's bad, or at least 'feigning utter indifference' cop. As someone who had been in Ravensbury House at the same time as Dr Pitkin the previous evening, I was already on their list of people to talk to, and as I was the one who had found a knife, I was now officially a witness and the blade my exhibit. None of which was as exciting or interesting as it sounds; the questions were simple, confirming the order of events during the evening, who had been there, what contact I'd had with the victim. Did I see Dr Pitkin leave? Did I see anyone suspicious?

Away from the comfort of Charleton House and the familiar faces of DC Joe Greene and DS Colette Harnby, the Derbyshire police detectives who had been involved in every other case I'd paid attention to, I found the whole process a little staid and businesslike. But that could have been something to do with the personalities of the detectives involved. I'd become very comfortable around the police in Derbyshire, taking for granted that a cup of coffee and a chocolate brownie could help me find out a little more about their investigations than I was entitled to know. I also missed the banter that I shared with Joe and the friendship that was developing with Harnby. Here, I had to accept that I wasn't anything special, just a witness in a long line of witnesses whose name would now go in a file. This was one crime that Sherlock Sophie and her duo of Watsons – also known as Mark and Joyce – would not be solving.

CHAPTER 6

The team had no opportunity to be distracted while they worked. As soon as it was confirmed that each person hadn't been around last night, the police said they could go. The house was going to be searched and it would take most of the day, so it made sense for them to leave and not return until the following morning. I was allowed to remain and continue with my job, and was loath to leave, but what Joyce had said was spot on: I was distracted and had to make multiple attempts at finishing a rota for the team. This time, I couldn't even blame a lack of coffee.

I was putting my laptop away and preparing to go when the Duke wandered into the café, looking lost. I realised it was the first time I had ever seen him with his hands in his pockets.

'Ah, Sophie, is all well?' He looked aimlessly around the room. I could have told him that I'd ordered some llamas for the garden and my staff had all agreed to work topless, and I doubt he'd have noticed.

'Fine, thank you. Can I help with anything?'

'Hmm, no thank you, I had one earlier.'

I waited a moment while he examined the spines of the books on the shelves.

'I was sorry to hear about Dr Pitkin, he seemed like such a nice man.'

'Indeed he was.'

'But then, no life should be lost just for the theft of a wallet.'

'No. What? Oh, he wasn't robbed. The police said he still had his wallet and laptop on him. It seems this wasn't a robbery that went awry.'

I wasn't expecting to hear that. 'So he was killed on purpose? He was the target?'

'It seems that way.'

The Duke sat in one of the armchairs and crossed a leg over the other, revealing green socks covered in pineapples. He noticed me staring.

'A gift from Evelyn. She thought they were funny and matched the palm room. Always marry someone with a sense of humour, Sophie; life isn't worth living without it.' The mention of life and its worth sent us into what felt like a painfully long silence. I still couldn't quite understand why the Duke was here with me and I was grateful when he started talking again.

'I can't even begin to think why someone would want to kill him. He was very well regarded in his field, and a genuinely nice man. A touch eccentric perhaps, but I found that rather charming. It's a shame we don't have the likes of Detectives Greene and Harnby to talk to. We immediately know so much more when this sort of thing happens in Derbyshire.'

'Can't the police here tell you anything?'

'Very little. You might say information is being shared on a need-to-know basis only; they certainly aren't the kind to let anything slip, so I can't imagine I'll get many updates. I have no doubt you could find out more, Sophie, and possibly a lot more quickly than I.'

I tried to work out the expression on his face. If he was wanting to tell me something, I couldn't translate it.

'Perhaps you might consider… I'm sure you could find a reason to… you're very good at asking questions…'

'What? Sort of… what? Oh!' Was the Duke really asking me to look into the death of his friend? I found it hard to believe, but as I watched him, he stopped staring into the distance and looked intently at me. 'You want me to…?'

'Well, not exactly. It's just… I'd like to know *something* and those detectives aren't going to give anything away. You do seem to have quite a knack for this kind of thing. Mind you, murders have a tendency to occur when you are around. Forgive my being blunt, but are you cursed?'

The beginnings of a smile appeared. I noted it was the second time that day the idea of a curse had been attached to me. I thought about my friends in the Derbyshire Constabulary; they never entirely approved of my habit of getting involved in murder investigations, but they had come to accept I had my uses and was able to gather information that they might not have access to. Not everyone was keen to talk to the police.

'I could ask a few questions. The detectives here won't be on the lookout for that, unlike DS Harnby who always has half an eye on what I am up to.'

'True, but I'd be careful if I were you. The detectives I met were much less, shall we say, affable than our sergeant. It might be advisable to stay out of their way if at all possible.' I took this as a friendly warning. After my brief experience of Grey and Knapp, I agreed with everything the Duke said.

'Do you mind if I ask more about your link to Dr Pitkin?' I enquired.

The Duke relaxed back in the armchair. 'The only link is Caroline, my great-great-aunt. Ambrose – Dr Pitkin – told you a little about her. Ambrose is – was – a botanist, and he enjoyed botanic art as well. He took an interest in her work and approached me for access to some of her paintings. We met a handful of times and got on extremely well. He would send me papers he had written about her, tell me when he had found more of her paintings, which I would invariably go on to buy in order to add them to the collection. And then he approached me to ask if I would donate them to the archives of the Natural History Museum. Of course, I agreed.'

'Was that contentious in any way?'

'Not in the slightest.'

'Are you aware of him having any disputes, professional or otherwise?'

The Duke thought for a moment; he seemed to have perked up a little now he was engaged in conversation. He shook his head.

'You'd need to talk to his colleagues at the Natural History Museum about that sort of thing. There's the ongoing banter between Gideon and myself, but that's more friendly than anything.'

'Go on,' I said encouragingly.

'Gideon Snable-Bowers, the Earl of Baxworth, also had a botanically inclined ancestor, his great-great-uncle, Jacob Snable-Bowers. There is some evidence that Caroline and Jacob met on their travels. Sadly, Jacob died on one of his trips, and Gideon is convinced that Caroline laid claim to some of his discoveries.'

'And how do you feel about that?'

The Duke laughed and waved his hand in the air as though swatting away a fly.

'The man's a fool. I set no store by it. He also claims that my grandfather is the reason his family is penniless. They possess only their titles and he lives in rented accommodation.'

'Why does he think your relative is to blame?' I wasn't sure if the Earl's links to the Duke were relevant, but the subject had caught my interest.

'His father was a drinker and a gambler. He made a series of incredibly bad business decisions that left the family bankrupt, and simultaneously lost a lot of money at cards, to the benefit of my grandfather. I don't believe the 10th Duke of Ravensbury ever lost a game in his life.'

'So the Earl of Baxworth has plenty of reasons to be annoyed at your family, but I'm not sure why that would be important.'

'Oh, none of it is serious. We get on well. Besides which, he has to maintain a good relationship with our circle if he wants any of us to sign him in as a guest at his favourite clubs. It would be rather foolish of him to start damaging relationships.' I agreed, but maintaining a positive relationship with Dr Pitkin was less important. The link between the two men seemed rather tenuous, but it was a start.

'Ambrose wanted to talk to me, you know; asked for a meeting to be added to the diary for today. I should be having a cup of tea with him around now; instead, the poor chap is dead.'

'Do you know what he wanted to discuss with you?'

'No idea, but it wasn't like him to make an appointment; generally, he'd just raise a subject when we were together. You should talk to Molly, he asked her to schedule the meeting. They got on rather well, so he might have told her.'

He paused before looking me in the eye.

'Of course, I can't be seen to encourage you to do any of this.'

'Don't worry. If anyone asks, we've simply been discussing your socks.'

CHAPTER 7

I found it impossible to enter the Natural History Museum without stopping and gazing at the vast cathedral to nature. After walking under the magnificent arches and into its main hall, I was greeted by the skeleton of a blue whale that appeared to be swimming through the air before me. It was impressive, but not what drew my attention. Instead, it was the ceiling, covered in paintings of plants that spoke of the role of the country in the discovery and mapping of flora across the world, its steel frame exposed like its own skeleton; the terracotta tiles on the walls; the carved animals and birds that crawled up columns.

The grand staircase led to a statue of Charles Darwin, who watched over schoolchildren as their jaws dropped in awe and adults who, like me, would never forget the first time they stepped into this wonderland so many years ago. I'd spent hours exploring this building over the years, and many more in the cafés with Zannah, putting the world to rights and attempting to fix our fragile love lives. There had been a time when the staff on the reception desk recognised me, but not anymore. I didn't see a single familiar face.

'Sophie, Mark,' Zannah called over the heads of some young children in matching hi-vis vests. 'Come on, let's get away from the hordes. I love children… barbecued.' That last word wasn't in the slightest bit true. I'd watched Zannah as she worked with children in the Explorer Centre, where school groups went for their lessons; there wasn't an age range she couldn't win over.

With a coffee each and a packet of shortbread bites to share, we relaxed into the familiar surroundings. In the café at the far end of the hall, we were surrounded by terracotta archways, the floor made of tiny tiles. We could be looked down upon from a balcony that surrounded us on four sides, archways all the way along. It was another religious space, one that felt slightly Moorish, and I wouldn't have been surprised to hear a call to prayer.

I savoured my first mouthful of coffee, watched intently by my friends.

'It's good to see some things haven't changed,' Zannah said, her voice lightly teasing.

'Did she have that rusty coffee grinder when she lived down here?' asked Mark.

'Yes, she did. Now, are you going to tell her, or shall I?' Zannah dropped her voice to a conspiratorial whisper and cupped a hand round her mouth to direct it at Mark. 'You can buy it ready ground.'

'Oh, stop it, you two. I've never heard either of you complain when I make you a cup of coffee, and my grinder is not rusty. It's the patina of age, or something. But it's perfectly good and perfectly hygienic.'

Zannah and Mark looked at each other sympathetically; introducing them to one another wasn't proving to have been such a good idea. After another sip of reasonably good coffee, I turned to Zannah.

'Have you heard?'

'About Ambrose, yes. The news spread around this place like wildfire.'

'How did you find out so quickly?' Mark asked.

'I think they'd struggle to find any family members, and the only contact details he was likely to have had on him, or if the police did some kind of search of his home, are for this place. They called Caleb, his head of department.'

I hadn't spoken much to Dr Caleb Orne last night, but I did remember being surprised by how young he looked.

'We don't know what happened, though, simply that he was found dead in Green Park this morning. Do you know any more? We assumed that he was robbed as he walked home.' I glanced down at my coffee. 'You do know more, don't you, Sophie?'

'It looks like he was targeted. Whoever killed him didn't take anything from him. He still had his wallet and laptop on him.'

'Really?' Zannah's eyes bulged. 'Poor Ambrose, who could want to hurt him? That's awful.' She paused and I let her take a minute for the information to sink in.

'Don't worry,' said Mark. 'Sophie'll have it solved by the end of the day and it will once again be safe to walk the streets of London. She seems to attract murder like bees to honey. I don't know why I thought we could have a drama-free trip to the big city.'

He took a sip of coffee and looked as if the case was closed. Zannah stared at me with her head cocked, her eyes drilling into me. It was remarkable; even when silent, she emitted an impressive level of energy.

'In some of your emails, you've mentioned a few police investigations at Charleton House. Were you a little more involved than you let on?'

'Involved?' Mark cried out. 'She's Derbyshire's answer to Miss Marple, she wears a deerstalker hat to work and she's currently trying to cultivate a moustache to rival Poirot.' I thumped him, and then ran a finger along my top lip. Was it time to get the hair removal cream out? 'If she carries on, they're going to be making staff cutbacks in the Derbyshire police; they won't be able to justify having any detectives at all.'

'Have you finished?' I scolded him. 'Take a breath, drink your coffee. I have...' How was I going to describe it? *Solved a few murders* just sounded crazy '...been able to help the police with their enquiries from time to time.'

Zannah looked at Mark. 'I take it that's an understatement?' He nodded with a look of incredulity. Her face lit up. 'Fantastic! Well, I'm in; what do we do first?'

'We don't do anything.' I thought about my conversation with the Duke; I had said I would ask a few questions, but I didn't like the idea of getting my friend involved. On the other hand, she was perfectly placed to help.

'Come on, please. I've missed you, it would be great to work with you on this.' She looked pleadingly at me. I sighed.

'Alright. I guess there would be no harm, but you have to be careful, this is serious. There's a killer out there, and even if they only wanted to silence Dr Pitkin, they might not be concerned about doing the same to someone who gets too close to working out their identity.'

Zannah leant back in her chair and clapped her hands together. Mark simply shook his head and reached for another shortbread bite. Talking about murder was no longer something that caused the slightest raise of an eyebrow from him.

'So where do we start?' Zannah queried.

'With you, as it happens.'

'Me? Why me?'

'Because you knew him, you worked in the same building and you're sat right in front of me.'

'I didn't work with him often; I just coordinated opportunities for him to engage with school groups and give talks.'

'Doesn't matter. What do you know about him? Anything – it can be factual or gossip, but it'll give us something to start with.'

'Okay, well, he was a nice bloke. I know he looked like the

stereotypical scientist that you'd expect to find in the corner of an old-school laboratory, bent double over an antique microscope and lacking in all social skills, but he wasn't like that. Always very happy to advise us when we were developing new school activities. There are some scientists who find dealing with anything outside the lab a rather tiresome part of the job they can't avoid, but he really got involved. He was a little unusual, but not shy.'

'Unusual how?'

'In his own world, I guess you'd say. He'd disappear into his thoughts in the middle of a conversation, and then start talking like you knew what he'd been thinking. It was always related to what you had been discussing, but it took some getting used to. People who didn't know him could think he wasn't paying any attention to them when the opposite was true: he was taking what they said seriously. He often worked late. I've seen him setting off for home on his bicycle at all sorts of hours. I was here for an event once and I watched him leave at eleven o'clock. Security told me that wasn't unusual. What else? Oh yes, his house is like a museum.'

'You've been to his house?'

'No, but my friend Tess Little has, and dozens of others. He had his own collections and used to invite colleagues round to see his latest acquisition.'

'Come and see my etchings?' Mark looked deeply suspicious.

'It wasn't like that,' Zannah reassured him. 'He had garden parties in the summer, although I'm told his garden was more like an Amazonian jungle and you needed a machete to hack your way round it. He also held classes there. Tess said his home looked like something out of the 19th century, all heavy wooden cabinets with glass doors and floor-to-ceiling bookcases. She could never work out where he would relax. There was no TV and the fridge was always empty.'

'Did Tess work with him?'

Zannah nodded. 'She's an administrator in the Botany Department.'

'What about his other colleagues? What did they think of him?'

She thought for a moment. 'Poor Caleb.' She shook her head. 'I bet he feels awful now.'

'Why?' I asked.

'As they were leaving work yesterday, I saw him and Ambrose have an almighty row. I think they were waiting for a taxi, just outside the staff entrance. Caleb stormed off and Ambrose jumped in the taxi when it arrived. Imagine your last real conversation with someone being a fight.'

I looked over at Mark. 'They seemed fine later at Ravensbury House,' I commented.

'We only saw them briefly, and yes, they were being perfectly polite. But they might not have said much to each other directly all evening, so they could have been simmering with anger underneath it all.'

'Anyone else, Zannah? Any other colleagues who might hold strong views on Dr Pitkin?'

'You'd have to ask Tess.'

'Do you think she'd talk to me?'

'Yes, definitely. I haven't been able to get hold of her this morning, but I know his death will have hit her hard. She's the type that gets quite attached. She knows the birthdays of everyone in the department and they all get a card. At Easter, she puts a little chocolate egg in everyone's pigeonhole. I haven't heard her say a bad word about anyone. I should really make an effort to go and find her after this.'

'One more thing: can you think of anyone who would want him dead?'

She immediately shook her head. 'I've no idea, but I'd like to help you find whoever did this.'

With that, she gave Mark and me a hug, and then disappeared through a door marked *Private*.

CHAPTER 8

As Mark and I walked out of the museum and back into the sunshine, I watched a couple of children running on the grass in front of the building. One carried a plastic dinosaur, which he dropped before quickly turning back to retrieve it.

'Mark, something doesn't quite make sense. Why would the murder weapon be up by Ravensbury House? Dr Pitkin died in the park. Either he was stabbed near the house and managed to make his way to the park, or the murderer came from a different direction, killed him in the park, and their escape route took them past the house where they dropped the weapon. And if Dr Pitkin had been stabbed up at the house, then surely someone would have seen him staggering along.'

'Not necessarily. He might not even have realised that he'd been stabbed.'

'Seriously? That happens?'

'Empress Elisabeth of Austria was stabbed in the heart with a pointed file. She actually thought she had been punched, went on to board a ship – she walked on having no idea what had happened. She eventually collapsed, and that was when they realised the extent of her injuries. I'm sure Joe could tell you about some modern examples.'

'Thanks, but I won't tell him about all this. Not yet, anyway.'

'So yes, it's perfectly plausible for Dr Pitkin to have been stabbed near the house, then walked away blissfully unaware and collapsed when he got to the park.'

'I don't know whether not knowing would have been better or worse for him. It must have been confusing and frightening in a whole different way.'

'Well, let's just hope it was quick.'

I was deep in my thoughts when I walked into a wall; or at least, it felt like a wall. I looked up to apologise and found myself staring into the eyes of gym-bunny Detective Sergeant Knapp. He took a step backwards.

'Sorry, madam. Oh, Miss… Lockwood?'

'Yes, Sophie Lockwood.'

'And you're here because?' enquired his less friendly partner, Detective Inspector Grey.

'The dinosaurs,' Mark replied with a straight face. 'The Triceratops is my favourite, but you should see the roaring T-Rex; I still think it's pretty scary.' I could have sworn that I saw the corner of DS Knapp's mouth twitch in the direction of a smile. He nodded and they continued towards the museum entrance.

'You're not going to be able to bribe him with a chocolate croissant or endless cups of coffee,' Mark warned.

'What are you saying about my chocolate croissants? That they can't compare with their London cousins?'

'I know they compare very favourably because you have them made at a London bakery. Anyway, DS Muscles probably consumes nothing but protein shakes and rare steaks to bulk him up. All I'm saying is if you do want to look into all of this, then you're on your own; there'll be no inside information slipping out accidentally during pleasant chit chat.'

I knew he was right, but fortunately, I rather enjoyed a challenge.

'Do you think it might be linked?' Zannah asked as she handed me the tub. We'd opted for an early night with pyjamas and some rather indulgent salted caramel swirl ice cream. Penny was sitting next to me, so close I could feel her pressing against my leg. I knew her interest was purely of the dairy kind, so I let her lick a little off the end of my finger. Her permanently perturbed expression didn't change, but she rubbed her snub nose against my arm, so I assumed she was happy.

I shrugged. 'I don't see how.'

'If the Earl of Baxworth does want to get his own back on the Duke, but is wise enough not to attack the Duke directly, then he might feel the need to make one of his supporters suffer.'

'His supporters?' I laughed. 'This isn't the Tudor period, with allegiances and grudges passed from generation to generation.'

'I don't know about that. Royalty, aristocratic families: it's all pretty archaic by its very nature.'

'You becoming anti-royal on me?' I passed the tub back.

'When have you ever known me to get excited by a royal wedding, or another sprog born with a silver spoon in its mouth? But no, I'm not anti-royal, I just think it all needs modernising. Even a little will do.'

She had a good point, but I wanted to get her back on track.

'But what does the Earl actually gain by killing Dr Pitkin?'

'Well, it's not going to bring back the family wealth, but it would mean there was one less person talking about Caroline and taking the attention away from his ancestor. He might have been overtaken by anger and frustration. He'd just heard Ambrose talking about this amazing woman and all her wonderful achievements, and he must have been fuming as his family once again gets sidelined and their role in important scientific discoveries erased from history.' Zannah shrugged as she finished. 'Just an idea.'

Penny's eyes were watching the spoon as it travelled from the tub to Zannah's mouth and back again. She looked as if she was watching a tennis match.

'Why is she not hassling you?' I asked.

'She knows I won't give her any; I'm not a soft touch like you. How is that tabby elephant of yours? Do you damage your back when you pick her up?'

I scrolled through my messages and came to one Bill had sent me earlier in the evening. Bill, Mark's husband, had agreed to take Pumpkin in and look after her in my absence, and I showed Zannah the attached photo of my sizeable cat. Bill had fastened a small bow tie around her neck and she was sitting at the table; she had her own place setting and what appeared to be a plate of torn up chicken in front of her. How he'd managed to get her to sit still and not dive on the food as soon as it appeared, I had no idea.

'Bill does know that she's a she, right?'

'I guess he plans on making her the first feline drag king. I think it suits her; I just hope she didn't scratch his hands to shreds as he put it on her.'

Zannah handed me the phone back. 'Look, if you're serious about looking into this, then we need to meet up with Tess. She can give you more background on Ambrose; she might even know who else could have had it in for him.' She immediately starting tapping on her phone. 'I'll ask her if we can meet away from the museum, it might be safer. Preferably in a crowded place where no one knows us.'

'We're not Russian spies, I just want to find out more about his work, anything going on in his department.'

Zannah ignored me as her fingers flew over the screen of her phone. She poured enthusiasm into everything she did, and this was clearly going to be no different. I sat quietly, stroking Penny as a text message conversation took place.

'She's part-time and has the day off tomorrow, but could meet us early for coffee. I've messaged my own colleague; I don't have any meetings, but I've told him I'll be in by lunch and he'll cover for me until then. Tess might even have come across the Earl or know something about him that could help.'

I hoped I wasn't making a big mistake. I wasn't on 'home turf', as some might call it, and I didn't want to get Zannah or Tess into any trouble. But I couldn't escape the curiosity that had taken firm root inside me. It also seemed that there might be a historical connection, and thanks to Mark, I was increasingly enjoying delving into the archives of Charleton House. It had given me an appetite for investigating the past as well as the present.

CHAPTER 9

Despite the early hour, Borough Market was buzzing with people keen to get their fill of organic vegetables, freshly baked bread and pastries, and fish caught that morning in British waters. They could pick up Middle Eastern meze, Bao buns, or a grilled raclette cheese sandwich. If I'd wanted oysters for breakfast, I could have had them; if I wanted to leave with a jar of honey from beehives on the top of London city buildings, it was there for me to buy.

When I'd lived in London, Borough Market had been a favourite haunt of mine, a smorgasbord of stalls tucked under a crisscross of iron arches that formed railway viaducts, the sound of trains thundering overhead adding to the atmosphere. It was here that we had agreed to meet Tess, yards from the banks of the Thames and where I could get a sublime cup of coffee. I wasn't the only one who felt this way; the queue for the coffee roasters, with a little café attached, always snaked down the road, but it was worth the wait.

Zannah and I each had a cup and a warm pastry in our hands by the time we spotted Tess. We all hugged, and then started to meander among the stalls. Tess was like a little bird with thin limbs and eyes that darted around, taking everything in. Just like Zannah, she was full of energy, but hers was calmer. She reminded me of a ballet dancer in the wings of a theatre, waiting to leap on stage. Zannah, on the other hand, was a jungle of live wires buzzing all over the place.

'Thanks for meeting me here. I've promised I'll make dinner for my brother tonight, and I want to get the ingredients before I go over to look after my nephew for the day. I know that once I'm there, I'll never get to the shops.'

Once her hessian bag was overflowing and we'd queued for even more coffee, Tess led the way down to the water, past Southwark Cathedral where Shakespeare's brother was buried.

'Ambrose was a bit of an enigma,' Tess was explaining in between mouthfuls of fresh cherries. 'He could be quiet at times, didn't say a lot in meetings – which I liked as it made minuting them easier for me. A little absentminded, but he was fiercely passionate about his work and talking to others about it, sometimes regardless of whether or not they wanted to hear about it.'

We'd seated ourselves on a concrete bench looking across the Thames. The water was a muddy brown, but light danced across its surface and made it look less murky.

'You know about his parties, Zannah. It was just open house, he seemed to trust everyone and he wanted to share his interests.'

'He sounds so inoffensive,' I said, dusting pastry crumbs off my jeans. 'Did he not get on anyone's nerves; argue with someone who stole his milk from the staff fridge; anything at all?'

'Well, that's the thing. For all his mild-mannered ways, he could get stuck into things that were contentious. He certainly got some people's backs up, and he just wouldn't let go. It was as though he didn't notice that people were getting annoyed with him.'

'What kind of thing?' I asked. She paused, looking as if she was working hard to remember details.

'There was a case of suspected fraud, years ago. I'm talking the 1930s. A botanist, Roger Ferguson, who was very respected at that time, claimed to have found some plant life on the coast of Scotland – plant life which had only ever been found in the south of England until this discovery. This was revolutionary in terms of our understanding around Ice Age Britain. But one of his colleagues, Professor Ronald Judd, was convinced that something was wrong. I have no idea if these two had any sort of history of disagreements, but something made Professor Judd go and check. After some searching, he found the plants that Ferguson had discovered, but he realised they weren't native to the area and there was evidence that they had been moved. Later, more evidence of fraud was found.'

'And that was Ferguson's career over?' asked Zannah.

'Actually, no. The whole thing was buried by the London School of Botanical Studies that Ferguson worked for. Judd's report was also buried and there were strict instructions that it should never be mentioned again until after Ferguson's death.'

'So how is this related to Dr Pitkin?' I asked.

'Ambrose was keen to bring it all up again. Ferguson carried out a lot more work before he died, much of it very questionable, but he was well liked and no one seemed to regard it as an issue. And when Ambrose was raising the matter again, it was considered old news, a storm in a teacup that did no real lasting damage. I know the department at the museum didn't want to spend time and money on an issue that was no longer considered worth it. Ambrose had other projects to work on, but he was like a dog with a bone. I think other people in the department just got fed up with it.'

So, he was tiresome and irritating, I thought. *Hardly a good motive to kill someone.*

'I'm sorry, girls, I have to head off. My nephew will be driving his mum crazy if I'm late. I can guarantee he'll be in the window, watching for me as I arrive. I hope I've helped.'

'You have, thanks, Tess.' She really had. I felt like I was starting to get a much better picture of Dr Ambrose Pitkin.

Tess set off towards the station on the far side of the market, and Zannah and I walked along the Thames path towards Shakespeare's Globe and the Tate Modern, Zannah practically skipping alongside me.

'Right then, what's next?' she asked. 'Surely we need to find out more about the Ferguson fraud case, that might be key. What's your next move?'

'Telling you to take a breath and slow down.' I laughed. 'I don't want you getting into any trouble by ruffling feathers at the museum, so just keep your ear to the ground and let me know if you hear anything interesting that might be useful. I want to know more about…'

I was interrupted by the ringing of my phone. *Joe Greene* was written large across the screen.

'Good morning, Detective Constable,' I said cheerily, having put the call on speaker. Zannah opened her eyes wide at me and mouthed *Joe* while using her hands to form a heart shape. I glared at her.

'You sound chirpy. How's life in the Smoke? You causing chaos in the capital?' he asked.

'You've heard, then?'

'Of course I've heard. You haven't even been there forty-eight hours and they're zipping someone into a body bag.'

'The Duke has already raised the issue of my apparent curse.'

'And well he might. He's probably got a good case if he wants to fire you. Everywhere you go, a corpse is sure to follow; it's not good for any business. I hope you're enjoying the city, though, visiting a few museums, going shopping with Joyce. In other words, doing anything except attempting to investigate a murder.'

We'd reached the Tate Modern and I knew that Zannah needed to head off at this point and get back to the museum.

'One minute, Joe.' I gave my friend a hug.

'I expect you to tell me everything,' she whispered, pointing at the phone.

'I will.'

I watched her walk across the front of the large brick power station which now housed one of the finest modern art collections in the world, dodging tourists taking photos as she went, and then refocused on my phone.

'Sorry, Joe, I'm back.'

'No worries. Look, I know I tell you this all the time, but you really ought to stay out of this one. The Met is a whole different kettle of fish to us local yokels back in Derbyshire.' I heard him mutter something. 'Hang on, Soph, I'm putting you on speakerphone. The boss is here.'

I heard a change in sound quality, followed by the familiar voice of Detective Sergeant Colette Harnby.

'Sophie, Joe's right. Stay out of it. I've not had much contact with the Metropolitan Police, but you'll find them less forgiving than us. Not even the Duke is going to find a sympathetic ear, let alone you. You won't be able to bribe any of the detectives with coffee and cake in exchange for information.' I knew this comment would be accompanied by a rather pointed look in Joe's direction; I couldn't get Harnby to accept a free filter coffee when I *wasn't* digging for information, she was such a stickler for the rules. Joe was a different matter altogether. 'Have you met them yet?'

'Yes, I was interviewed. They don't seem very friendly.'

'Assume that they aren't, ever. Get on with your day job and spend any spare time you have shopping for fridge magnets in the shape of a London bus. There's nothing we or the Duke can do if you annoy the detectives working on the case. Have I made my point?'

'Very clearly,' I said, pausing for effect. 'Have you any way of finding out what their favourite cake is?'

'SOPHIE!' they shouted simultaneously.

'Just kidding. Yes, I've heard you; yes, I'll go shopping.' But I imagined them being quietly pleased that I was poking around the activities of the Met, and Derbyshire's wasn't the only police force subjected to my inquisitive nature. They might even be rather pleased if I solved the case first.

'Good. I'll leave you with Joe, some of us have work to do.'

I heard another change of sound quality as Joe took me off speakerphone.

'You're going to stick your nose in, aren't you?'

'You heard me. I'll do as I'm told and go shopping.'

'In between hacking off the Metropolitan Police. I know you, Sophie. Just be careful.'

'Always.'

CHAPTER 10

Mark, Joyce and I were gathered around the cash desk in the shop.

'Whoever it was had to know where Dr Pitkin would be on Tuesday night, which means it must be someone who was at Ravensbury House with him, or had access to his diary,' I mused.

'Or simply knew him well enough to say, "What are you doing tonight?"' Joyce added.

I turned to Mark. 'Can you try and find out more about Caroline Fitzwilliam-Scott and the Earl of Baxworth's claim that she took credit for one of his ancestor's discoveries? See if there's anything in it. I still think it's a bit tenuous that he would kill Dr Pitkin over it, but we can't rule him out, and a bit of research is right up your street.'

'We should start with Annabelle.'

'Our Duke's daughter?'

'Yes, she's named after Caroline Annabelle, and based on what I know of her personality, she'll have read about her great-great-great – is that right? Yes, great times three aunt.'

'Can you find out if she's up for a coffee?'

He nodded.

'And what am I? Window dressing?'

'Don't worry, Joyce, we are going to put your natural talents to use. I want you to sweet-talk the pants off… I mean, charm as much information as you can out of Gideon Snable-Bowers tonight.'

'And if he's not actually the guilty party, you never know, you might bag yourself an eligible titled bachelor,' Mark added.

'Thank you for that suggestion, Mark, but if I'm going to "bag", as you so delicately put it, someone with a title, I'd quite like them to have the family fortune that generally comes with it.'

I felt buoyed by the idea of us pooling our skills and momentarily forgot the sadness around Dr Pitkin's death.

My good mood drained out of me as I walked from the shop into the hallway. The two detectives were standing at the bottom of the stairs, talking to Molly. She was looking at a photograph, but glanced up as I entered.

'Sophie, good timing; these detectives would like to talk to you.' I swallowed hard, wondering if they'd found out about me asking questions. But I'd only spoken to Zannah and Tess, so that was unlikely.

I calmed down as Detective Sergeant Knapp took the photograph from Molly and handed it to me, his jacket straining against his broad shoulders and thick upper arms.

'We have a CCTV image of someone talking to Dr Pitkin not far from here on Tuesday just after eleven o'clock at night. It's not great, but we were wondering if it rang any bells. Did you see anyone like this outside when you arrived for work or when you left that evening?' The photograph was a black and white still from a CCTV camera, a view of the alleyway where I'd found the knife. The glare from a nearby light had caused a lot of the image to be whitewashed, but one of the figures in the shot looked very much like Dr Pitkin. The figure opposite him had on a dark hoodie, the hood pulled up. There was no sign of aggression; they just seemed to be talking. It was impossible to tell whether the figure was even male or female, let alone identify any more distinguishing features. It could have been almost anyone, and certainly wasn't familiar to me.

I shook my head.

'Sorry, I don't recognise them.' Detective Inspector Grey reached out to take the photo from me. I couldn't help but notice that his nails were rather dirty. He also had a face that my father would have described as looking like a bulldog sucking a thistle. He clearly wasn't interested in even trying to put people at ease.

He passed the photo to Mark, and then to Joyce.

'I wasn't here during the evening,' said Joyce.

'If you could take a look anyway, madam. They could have been in the area during the day.'

'Don't you have a better photo? This really isn't very good.'

'I'm sorry, madam,' said DI Grey, 'but we forgot to arrange to have a photographer stationed outside on the off chance of a murder.'

'There's no need to be...' I stood on her toe. 'Ow! What was that...'

'Are you...' Grey looked at his notes '...Joyce Brocklehurst, the gift shop manager?' I wondered how Joyce had been described to him in order for him to so quickly put two and two together.

'If you mean the Head of Retail for Charleton House and all associated sites, then yes, I am she. How can I be of assistance?' Despite the lack of any aristocratic blood in her veins, Joyce could sound like the lady of the manor when she wanted.

'Is there somewhere private we can go? We have some questions for you.'

'We can head to the shop, there won't be anyone in there. Sophie, you can come with us.'

'We only need to speak to you at this stage.'

'That may be so, but I am going to have Sophie accompany

me. I don't want to risk you planting drugs in my handbag while I'm distracted.'

'Madam, we are hardly... alright, let's get this over with.'

'Good luck,' said Mark to the detectives, who responded with looks of confusion. Or at least, I thought DI Grey looked confused somewhere behind his terminally irritated expression. Joyce led the way, the sound of her heels echoing in the entrance hall.

The four of us gathered about the desk that held the cash register.

'Do you recognise this?' The photo placed on the desk was of a knife with a long, narrow blade. The wooden handle was thin and engraved.

'Of course I do.' Joyce walked across the room to one of the displays of Charleton House gifts. 'Beautifully hand-crafted by someone only a few miles away from the house in Derbyshire especially for this exhibition.' She opened a long box and held a letter opener before us. 'See, this is the Fitzwilliam-Scott family crest inlaid into the handle, and along the blade, "Ravensbury House" has been engraved. Perfect for any stylish office.'

'A letter opener?' I tried to understand the connection, quickly realising what we were looking at. 'Was one of our letter openers the murder weapon? I didn't recognise it at the time.'

'It appears that way. Now then, Miss Brocklehurst...'

'Ms, if you don't mind.'

'My apologies.' DI Grey didn't sound very apologetic. 'We would be grateful if you could put together a list of everyone who has had access to these. I believe the exhibition is not yet open to the public, so that should keep the numbers down.'

'True, but there have been dozens of people in and out of here over the last couple of days. Anyone could have slipped in and taken one. It's going to take some time.'

The detective passed her a business card. 'If you could email the list to us by the end of the day.'

'We're opening the shop for this evening's reception, which means I'm going to be *very* busy. I can get it to you in the morning.'

'The end of today, please, *Ms* Brocklehurst. I suggest you make a start on it right away.'

It was rare to see a man not won over by Joyce's various charms; even gay men fell at her feet. It was sod's law that the one man who was clearly not enamoured by her had to be a Metropolitan Police detective inspector when we were paying more attention than he would like to his murder investigation. If he found out, then our usual charm offensive was already guaranteed to fail.

Joyce pursed her lips and dramatically pulled out a notepad and pen, glaring as she watched the detectives leave.

CHAPTER 11

Mark appeared in the doorway to the café as I was closing up.

'Can't you leave that to the others? Only Annabelle has just arrived and she's happy to talk about her namesake.'

He didn't need to ask twice.

Annabelle was out on the terrace, having a glass of champagne poured for her by a server in a plain white shirt and black skirt.

'I was able to convince the caterers to open a bottle for us. I've been in the office since 5am and I need a drink. I hope you don't mind.'

She handed us each a glass; I really didn't mind at all.

'Sophie, you look well. Being back in London seems to suit you.' Annabelle, the eldest of the Duke and Duchess's three children, looked very much like her mother. They both had impressive posture that made me feel like a true slouch, and were more on the handsome end of the spectrum than pretty. Annabelle, however, terrified me in a way her mother never had. I never wanted to cross the Duchess and had an inordinate amount of respect and admiration for her, but Lady Annabelle was a different matter. She was a solicitor, and I'd joked about her effect on witnesses in court, but she specialised in intellectual property and I had no idea if that even involved a courtroom. She was direct, frighteningly intelligent and polite in a way that made me think there might be a little sarcasm thrown in on occasion. Having said all that, she had become firm friends with Molly, who had assured me that Annabelle had spoken highly of me on a number of occasions, so I tried to focus on that.

'Mark tells me you would like to pick my brain about the marvellous Caroline. She's very much a favourite of mine; I really would give anything to have met her, although I believe she could be rather terrifying.'

A suitable namesake, then, I thought.

'She was in the rather fortunate position of having the money to pursue her hobby of searching out and drawing butterflies all over Europe, and it wasn't long before she became a very well-regarded lepidopterist and travelled much further afield: Southern and Eastern Africa, the Caribbean, USA, all over India. She wasn't just drawing them, she discovered a number of specimens. But it was when she had scientific papers published in the *Entomologist's Monthly Magazine* that she began to be taken much more seriously by the establishment.

'She returned to England to visit her family often, but didn't really live here; her home was out on the road, you might say. She was very close to her brother, the 9th Duke. He was quite a bit younger than her, but he was supportive of her work, although they were very different. He loved throwing parties; she would avoid social events like the plague. Is this the sort of thing you're interested in?'

'It is; it's great to build up an image of her. Did she write a lot of letters, keep a diary?'

'She did indeed. I've read some of them; I believe they're still in the archives at Charleton. What are you interested in finding out?'

'Do you know anything about her connections with Jacob Snable-Bowers?'

A smile spread across Annabelle's face as she lifted the glass to her lips. She took a sip before responding.

'Ah, the great Snable-Bowers clan. Yes, their paths did cross, in Uganda, or at least, that's where they ended up. Have you spoken to the Earl of Baxworth? He was here the other night, wasn't he?'

'He was, and I might speak to him later.'

'He's very proud of his family's history. You might want to double check anything he tells you, though.'

I noticed that Mark was making notes as he listened. He always had a notepad in his back pocket and that habit was paying off.

I pushed Annabelle for more. 'Can you tell us if there was anything about Jacob in Caroline's letters?'

She took another drink and thought for a moment. 'I don't remember a lot; I wasn't particularly interested in him, but I know he died in Uganda and that Caroline was there. She nursed him towards the end. It was the sleeping sickness that got him. There was an epidemic in 1901. Caused by a parasite, it starts with fevers and headaches, playing havoc with your sleep pattern. You can have tremors, some paralysis. The list of symptoms goes on and it's terribly unpleasant. They were in quite a remote area and he didn't get the treatment he needed.'

'Were they a couple?' Mark asked. Annabelle quickly shook her head.

'No. Caroline made it very clear in a number of diary entries that she wasn't the marrying kind.'

'What do you think of the Earl of Baxworth's theory that Caroline claimed some of Jacob's discoveries as her own?'

Annabelle frowned slightly as she pondered the question. 'I don't believe she did, but then I didn't do any in-depth research, so there is every chance he knows something I don't. However, as time went on, Caroline became more and more ambitious, so it could be that ambition caused her to take some short cuts. But would she take credit for someone else's discovery? I'm loath to believe it. One day, I ought to go through the archive and find out even more about the woman I'm named after. But that will have to wait until my retirement. Now, if you'll excuse me, I would like to get out of this suit and make a bit of an effort before tonight. It's lovely to see you both again.'

'What do you think?' I asked Mark after she'd gone inside.

'I think I should see what else I can find out. Perhaps Dr Pitkin found out something that would put paid to the Earl's claims of his ancestor being the true claimant to some of Caroline's discoveries. But then the Earl of Baxworth would also need to destroy the evidence, and I don't see how he could have done that. Nothing has been said about letters or diaries going missing. I'm struggling to see how this is related, and if we do find out something, we could just end up disappointing a family and be no closer to knowing who killed Dr Pitkin.'

I took off my glasses and stuck the end of a plastic arm between my teeth, nibbling on it as I thought. But the glass of champagne had already sent a few of my brain cells to sleep.

'You're probably right. Have a look into it anyway. I can't think of anything else right now.'

'Come on,' he said as he stood, 'let's go and freshen up. Maybe this evening will give you the distraction you need, let the old grey cells whir away in the background. Something will come to you.'

'I hope so, I'm stumped otherwise.'

'Early days, Miss Marple, don't give up yet.'

CHAPTER 12

A glass of champagne was offered to everyone who stepped in through the door, the simple entrance hall a deceptive welcome, giving no sign of what was to come. The richly decorated rooms with ornate architraves, gilded picture frames, and glittering candelabras could make you consider wearing your sunglasses indoors. All the furniture and artwork typically on display had been removed and replaced with items from Charleton House. Portraits of the Duke's ancestors pulled you into the story of the Fitzwilliam-Scott family, landscape paintings of their country home transported you to Derbyshire. Modern ceramics were placed next to Delft jars. The work of Rembrandt hung proudly next to that of Lucian Freud.

There was, however, one room that was always going to take centre stage and no piece of art stood a chance: the Palm Room. In here, columns had been turned into glittering carved palm trees, their branches stretching out across the walls. Marble statues of classical figures stood in each corner, gilded plasterwork lined the edge of the ceiling, and an enormous chandelier dominated the centre of the room.

'I like a bit of bling, but this is taking it too far,' muttered Joyce into my ear. I was briefly overwhelmed by her heavily floral perfume, a sure sign she was hoping to catch the eye – and nose – of a wealthy titled friend of the Duke. Either that or she was taking her role of interrogating Gideon Snable-Bowers very seriously. One look at her pale pink, figure-hugging dress, every stitch of which shimmered at the slightest movement, made me think of the words 'pot' and 'kettle'. She tottered off on her eye-watering heels, which also shimmered with each step.

Mark was giving small groups of people an introduction to each room, which afforded me the opportunity to soak up the atmosphere. This evening was a private viewing of the exhibition before it opened to the public, a chance for the Duke and Duchess to thank those who had helped make it possible.

The gathering of roughly fifty people had also become an impromptu memorial for Dr Ambrose Pitkin, whom the Duke had talked about in his welcome speech. Dr Caleb Orne, the Natural History Museum's Head of Botany, had also given a rather moving speech about the scientist's passion for his subject, adding a couple of very amusing stories about his eccentricities. The crowd included the staff who had set everything up and those who would keep everything ticking over at the house during the coming weeks, and it was lovely to see Chelsea in a rather nice pale blue summer dress with a glass in her hand, mingling with a confidence that surprised me. Fleur Lazarus appeared to be enjoying a conversation with one of the conservators who had travelled down from Charleton House with the paintings. Fleur had a loud, hearty laugh that made me think of posh private schools where the girls used expressions like 'jolly hockey sticks' and called each other Pongo and Piggers.

'You know, I'm really not comfortable with the idea of one of my letter openers being used as a murder weapon.' Joyce had reappeared by my side.

'Well there's not a lot you can do about it now.'

'I sent the list to that rather unpleasant detective this afternoon. There were thirty-five people whose names I could come up with and I'm waiting for a couple more. Quite how someone could untangle the identity of the killer from all that, I don't know.'

She was right. We needed to narrow down the suspects who had a connection to Dr Pitkin. The CCTV camera image showed that the most likely scenario was he knew his killer. I could only speculate that they had approached him as he left Ravensbury House, argued or had a conversation of some kind with him that left them very unhappy, stabbed him, and he walked away not knowing it had happened. Joyce was right, there was a long list of possible suspects, but I was sure the killer was known to Dr Pitkin, which would narrow things down. This wasn't just an opportunist who had been in the house by chance, picked up a souvenir letter opener and stumbled across Dr Pitkin later; this was someone who had a reason to be in the area that evening, or knew that Dr Pitkin would be there. Why else would they have pulled him aside in an alleyway so close to the house? Surely they would have waited in the park, or attacked him closer to home, or the museum?

I was convinced I could shorten that list of names.

'How's it going?' I asked Mark.

'A waste of time. I'm trying to show people around, but they keep seeing people they know and going off for a chat. I start with a group and end up with the lonely weirdo who decides they're my new best friend. I'm just going to hang around and be here to answer questions.'

'And enjoy the free drinks!'

'I'm not doing this for love alone.'

'I think you would. If you didn't have this job, you'd turn up uninvited at events and start dragging people around, imparting your knowledge.'

'You're probably right.'

'Have you seen Gideon Snable-Bowers? Joyce is on the prowl and we've not encountered him yet.'

'He's not coming. I asked the Duke; apparently that was why he was here the other night, to get a preview because he already had a commitment this evening.'

'Joyce will be disappointed.'

'You'll have to take her on a day trip. He's doing some work at the Chelsea Physic Garden, so I reckon you might be able to run into him there. If she needs any convincing, they have a very nice café.'

'Have you seen the way she's dressed? She won't need any convincing, she's a woman on a mission.'

'Again, Miss Marple, you're right. She'll probably... erm... I, er... more drink...' He walked off and I was left confused, wondering if he'd fetch me another while he was at it.

'Sophie.' I didn't need to turn around; I knew who the voice belonged to. I felt my stomach lurch. Closing my eyes, I took a deep breath before turning around.

'Adam.'

'I hoped you'd be here. You look great.'

I said nothing; he could carry the conversation. But I couldn't help notice how good he was looking, too; prison must have suited him, or at least kept him away from gourmet food.

He was six foot tall and had the physique of a man who could look trim and athletic without too much effort, if he really wanted. However, I knew he liked high-end wines a little too much, and he also enjoyed treats from the kitchen when he was at work. It was all the nibbling that had done for him, not enormous plates of unhealthy fare.

There was a little more grey in his hair than I remembered, but other than that, he didn't seem to have changed much. He'd always had an endearing boyish look about him which had been one of the things that had attracted me to him. The last time I'd seen him before Tuesday when I'd spotted him through the window at Dukes – and now I knew it was him I'd seen – he was being driven off in a police car. Defrauding the restaurant we both worked for of thousands of pounds had landed him a two-year prison sentence. This had all come after I'd walked in on him *in flagrante* with one of the servers in our bed, while I had been going about my business wearing his engagement ring. I considered myself over him, but I had no desire to see him again.

'Oliver invited me, and I knew the champagne would be good quality.' He grinned.

'And you know Oliver because…?'

'He's a regular in the restaurant I work at.' The awkward silence that followed must have lasted seconds, but it felt like forever. 'Look, I know you probably want nothing to do with me, but while you're in London, wouldn't it be nice to… I don't know, catch up? Bury the hatchet?' He handed me a business card. 'You don't have to say anything now, but call me. I'd love to go for a drink with you.' He smiled before walking away.

'Who's that fine figure of a man?' asked Joyce over my shoulder. I turned and stared at her, bug-eyed; I had shown both her and Mark pictures of my ex, which she could be forgiven for forgetting, but I wasn't feeling very forgiving. And Mark had clearly remembered as he'd slunk away as soon as he'd seen Adam approach, rather than get caught up in the inevitable awkwardness.

Luckily, Mark stepped in. 'That, my dear, is a man that none of us wants anything to do with. Am I right, Sophie?'

'Spot on.'

'Why? He looks like he'd be rather charming. I noticed him give you a card, Sophie, but if you don't want it, I'll happily…'

'Oh, for God's sake, woman, that's the ex who did time,' Mark stated firmly. Joyce paused, looking momentarily shocked before taking a sip of champagne.

'Well, that's him off my list, then. Mark dear, get the girl another drink, only see if they have something stronger. This is exquisite champagne, but an occasion like this calls for something more… numbing.'

CHAPTER 13

I'd managed to talk Joyce out of pouring a single malt whisky down my throat and convince her that I was fine. She was furious when I revealed I had already spotted Adam on the day we arrived and not told her, but I hadn't wanted anyone to make a big deal out of it. I knew how protective my friends could be, which was lovely, but could also be hard work.

After half an hour during which she wouldn't leave my side, she was eventually drawn away by a rather distinguished-looking gentleman. She'd overheard him being introduced as a baron and set her laser-like sights on him. I was faced with the perfect distraction when I saw Fleur Lazarus alone on the terrace, her glass almost empty. I quickly grabbed two champagne flutes from a server who was circulating with a tray of drinks and went to join her.

Fleur was stick-thin. Quite how she found the strength to climb Everest when she looked as though she'd get blown over in a strong wind, I had no idea. Her skin was tanned and had a slight leathery look to it, but it was skin that had been exposed to the toughest elements in the world rather than too much time on a sunbed. Her long blonde hair was streaked with grey and tied back in a ponytail; she didn't seem to be a woman who put much store by expensive salons.

'Ah, so you're the official Charleton House detective; Evelyn told me a little about you. It all sounds rather fascinating, and I do like a woman who is not prepared to watch things happen around her, but rather steps up to the plate and gets involved. I salute you.' She raised her glass to me and took a drink. 'Of course, the bottom line is that what's happened is really quite tragic.'

'Did you know Dr Pitkin?'

'No, not really. We both went to Oxford, but our paths never crossed. I studied geography. I knew he worked at the Natural History Museum, I'd seen his name crop up in one or two newspaper articles, and I'm often at the Royal Geographical Society around the corner from the museum, but I hadn't seen him. It's awful to think that he was killed as soon as he left here.'

'Did you see him that evening?'

'Yes, we were all leaving at a similar time. The Duchess walked me out as the Duke's group were getting ready to leave. I was introduced to them all, and then I left. I remember thinking how nice it was to see him and perhaps I'd run into him again. Sadly, that's not to be. I really don't understand how someone could want to kill a mild-mannered scientist. I'm used to death. You can't do the kind of expeditions I do and not be prepared for the worst; Mother Nature can be utterly brutal. But this... this is different.'

As she spoke, a number of people wandered out onto the terrace, one of whom recognised Fleur and came over to introduce herself. I left them to it and went back inside.

'Ah, Sophie, enjoying the chance to mingle rather than pour the wine?' The Duke smiled at me.

'I am indeed, thank you.'

'You met Caleb the other night?'

I shook hands with Dr Caleb Orne. 'Yes, lovely to see you again. That was a very nice speech you made about Dr Pitkin.'

'Thank you, I hope I did the man and his work justice.' Dr Orne looked to be in his early forties; his salt-and-pepper stubble and short, slightly untidy hair looked more like a fashion statement than laziness or the unintentional style of a distracted scientist. He wore a designer suit, not Savile Row expensive, but it was enough to make you do a double take. The lack of a tie and the creases in the shirt gave the outfit a slightly casual look. He seemed very comfortable in his skin and his surroundings, and I wondered what his background was.

'I envy you, working at the Natural History Museum; it's a beautiful building.'

Dr Orne looked around him. 'You're hardly in a concrete office block.' I laughed, embarrassed, and glanced at the Duke, who fortunately found my faux pas amusing.

'Yes, what are you trying to say, Sophie? Are our properties losing their shine for you?'

'No, no, I just meant...'

'Don't worry, you're right.' The Duke smiled. 'Alfred Waterhouse designed a most spectacular building. Even behind the scenes. The herbarium is a fascinating place. Have you ever seen it, Sophie?'

'No, never.'

'You must. Caleb, I'm sure you could arrange for Sophie to have a little glimpse into your world?'

'It would be my pleasure.' Dr Orne looked genuinely taken with the idea, rather than feeling obliged because one of the highest-ranking aristocrats in the country had suggested it. 'I was planning on dropping by the office on Saturday, would that work for you?' Like many, he clearly didn't realise that Saturday was a standard day of work for those in the service industries, but it was an opportunity I didn't want to miss. The museum was a thirty-minute walk away and I wouldn't be long.

'Great, I'll be there. Thank you.' I wasn't entirely sure if this had been an intentional ploy by the Duke to get me behind the scenes at the museum in order to find out more information about Dr Pitkin, but there was nothing about his demeanour to indicate that was the case, and I had always known him to be a generous and encouraging man, so it was in character in the most normal of circumstances.

After some small talk, Dr Orne and the Duke went on to circulate, and I went to find Joyce. There was bound to be a terrified man who needed rescuing from her clutches.

JOYCE WAS NOWHERE to be found, so I took the opportunity for a moment's peace and quiet and sat in the darkened café, scrolling through my phone. Bill had sent me a message to tell me that Pumpkin was fine and seemed to be rather partial to smoked salmon. I cursed the man; she was going to return to me with expensive tastes, and knowing Pumpkin, she'd go on hunger strike if I didn't meet her newfound dietary needs. I would, of course, cave almost immediately, and she'd spend the rest of her days eating a fancier menu than the Duke and Duchess.

'Hello, Sophie.' In the half light, I almost mistook Annabelle for her mother.

'Lady Annabelle, can I get you anything?'

'I have a craving for a cup of tea. Rather dull for a night like tonight, but it's been a long day and if I have any more champagne, I'll fall asleep.'

'Let me.' I leapt out of my seat.

'Sit. I'm perfectly capable.' She rooted around behind the counter. 'Glad to see you were given the chance to enjoy this evening rather than running around after everyone, although why are you hiding in here? The rabble getting a bit much? I don't blame you, needed to escape myself.'

Annabelle returned to the table with a mug of steaming tea,

which looked oddly out of place against the backdrop of her cream suit and chunky gold jewellery which I guessed was worth a fortune.

'I just needed a moment of...' I wasn't sure how to finish. I'd come for some quiet, but that would sound rude under the circumstances.

'A moment of peace? Rather stuffed that up, didn't I.' She laughed. 'Sorry about that, but I did want a word.' I couldn't begin to think what she might want to talk to me about. 'I saw you chatting to Oliver's friend – is it Adam?' I nodded. 'Do you know him well? Only it didn't look like the first time you had met.'

'I knew him when I lived in London, but we haven't had contact for some time.' *Because he's been in prison*, I said in my head.

'I was just curious, that's all, as he's not a familiar face.' I sensed she wanted me to say more, but as much as I had reason to dislike Adam, or even want revenge, it wasn't my place to be telling all and sundry about the developments in his life which had resulted in him spending time at Her Majesty's pleasure.

Annabelle took another drink of tea before placing her mug on the table and standing. 'Well, it's good to see you again, Sophie. I'm sure our paths will cross before you return to Derbyshire. I must find Molly and drag her away from the fray where she's been working her socks off. We're planning a weekend away and we need to book our flights soon, so I shall distract her for a little while with talk of travel.'

She strode out of the room, leaving me with the distinct feeling that there had been a definite purpose to our seemingly innocuous conversation. That and an empty mug for me to wash up.

CHAPTER 14

'Now, Zannah, tell me about this rotten fiancé of Sophie's.'

Mark, Joyce and I had come back to Zannah's for a post-reception wash-up meeting, also known as a drink away from the prying eyes of our employers. I had just stocked Zannah's drinks cabinet – the cupboard under the sink – as part of my thank you for having me to stay, and fancied making a start on that rather than going to a noisy pub. However, it was a strange feeling, having my two worlds collide like this. My old life in London felt a very long time ago, even though only two years had passed.

'Ex-fiancé,' I corrected.

Penny chose that moment to make an appearance. She jumped up on the coffee table and sniffed our drinks before Zannah gave her a gentle push off.

'What on earth?' gasped Joyce. 'Has that thing had an accident?' Penny turned, looking for all intents and purposes as if she understood what Joyce had said. With her flat face, she naturally looked displeased. 'Did she hurtle towards the cat flap only to discover it was locked?'

'Joyce! Don't be so cruel. She's adorable.' I watched with amusement as, just out of sight of Joyce, Penny started chewing on the straps of the stilettos that she had discarded on the floor. I decided not to say anything.

'Who's adorable?' asked Mark as he walked back into the room. 'Oh. My. God. She *is* adorable.' He swept Penny up into his arms. 'Well, hello there, kitty, and who might you be?'

'Err, Penny,' I replied, wondering who this strange man was. The Mark I knew hated Pumpkin with a passion, but then she hated him just as much so it was a well-balanced relationship.

'Penny the Persian, perfect. Well, you and I are going to become good friends.' He took a seat on the opposite end of the sofa from me, and after she had given his moustache a good sniff, Penny curled up on his lap. 'She's so light, like caramel candy floss.' He stroked her delicately, as though he was afraid she might break.

'You're not getting off that lightly, young lady. So, Zannah, this Adam chappie. Deserved to be kicked into touch, or a lost opportunity now the dust has settled?'

'Dust settled?' I exclaimed. 'He was sent to prison for defrauding the restaurant we worked at, and don't forget the waitress he was having his merry way with.'

'Fair enough,' she agreed. 'That would rather tarnish the romance.'

'There wasn't a lot of that, either,' I added.

'You're well shot of him, Soph,' said Zannah. 'He was a good laugh, but I actually thought he was a little boring. Shows just how wrong a girl can be. How are you feeling now you've spoken to him for the first time since... well...'

'Since I watched him being driven off in a police car?' I thought about it for a moment. 'I'm still a bit in shock. Not in an awful way, I knew there was a chance I'd run into him; I just didn't expect it to happen at Ravensbury House.'

'That was probably the best place it could have happened.' I looked over at Mark who was lovingly rubbing Penny's ears. 'She does like a good lug rub, don't you? Don't you?' He glanced up. 'Well, think about it: you had to stay calm, get on with your job. You were immediately distracted and had to just plough on. There was no time to overthink things or get emotional...'

'Plough on?' interrupted Joyce. 'A lady doesn't just plough on. Can't you come up with a more delicate metaphor, Mark?'

'I suppose you're right. I'm not sure what I would have done if it was just the two of us on the street or if he appeared out of nowhere and sat next to me on a bus.'

'And you couldn't stab him with a fork in his family jewels. Oh sorry, that was a bit insensitive, what with Ambrose having been stabbed.' Zannah looked embarrassed, but I laughed.

'I did want to do that for a long time. But enough time has passed, I'm not going to let him bother me anymore. I've moved on, moved away...'

'And now your life is filled with the joy of our company.' Mark grinned at me. 'Life up north really suits you, Sophie, you're back where you belong.'

'Hmm, you're not really in the north, though, are you? More like the Midlands.' There was a glint in Zannah's eye that I recognised. We'd had this playful argument many times and I wondered who would be the first to rise to the bait.

It was Mark. 'I'll have you know, young lady, Derbyshire is indeed in the north, not the Midlands, which is a ridiculous idea. The Midlands! I ask you. Since when has a compass had north, south, east, west and *the middle*? Ridiculous. We are also definitely north of Watford, which is where most Londoners think the country comes to a sudden and abrupt end. The day I have to pay ten quid for a pint in a Derbyshire pub is the day you can tell me I no longer live in the north. Okay, so that's a slight exaggeration, but it's about all sorts of things: costs of living, population density. I don't want to get too serious about this, so suffice it to say, I live in the *north*.'

'Well, that put me firmly in my place.'

'Oh, I wouldn't worry, Zannah.' Joyce looked at her sympathetically over her glass. 'I've seen arguments over that subject go on all night; you got off lightly. But do us a favour and don't mention it again, Sophie and I have to work with him.'

'My sincere apologies. I didn't mean to offend you, Mark.' Zannah filled up his glass.

'Apology accepted, and this will do nicely as a peace offering.' He took a long drink before returning to the head massage he was giving Penny.

'In the spirit of changing the subject,' I looked over at Mark, 'is there something going on with Oliver – the Duke's son?' I clarified for Zannah. 'Only Annabelle was asking who Adam was and I sensed there was something she wasn't saying.'

'Probably just being the protective big sister.' Mark didn't stop stroking Penny, or even look up. 'I get the impression she's taken it upon herself to try and protect her parents from any fallout from the wayward son. So far, so good, but I do think it's only a matter of time until we see him on the front of the *Daily Mail* with a "Lord Layabout the Lush Locked Up" headline.'

'Is he really that bad?'

'Nah, not really. He'll be on page eight down the bottom because he was involved in some business deal that fell apart and he now owes millions. He's more a chancer than a criminal. But the family can do without the negative press, so they all try and keep an eye on what he's up to.'

I wondered how they would feel about Oliver spending time with Adam if they knew the full story, but I didn't feel it was my place to tell them. It was a part of my life that I didn't want to intrude on my work.

Joyce leant across and filled up my glass. 'Get that serious look off your face and get your diary out, my girl. I want to schedule a shopping trip with you. We should make the most of our proximity to Oxford Street while we're here, and I've always said I want to help you update your wardrobe.'

I groaned and Mark sniggered. Any concerns about Adam disappeared immediately as I tried to think of excuses to avoid this particular version of hell.

CHAPTER 15

It was not uncommon for exhibitions to have a 'soft launch' a day or two before the official opening which was likely to bring in the crowds. This gave us the opportunity to test all our systems. Staff could get used to the way the ticket scanners worked without a queue snaking around the block, putting pressure on them, and learn how the public reacted to certain things. Were particular pictures more popular than we'd expected and the rooms that housed them likely to get overcrowded? Were the tills working properly?

I always enjoyed these days. The excitement of getting ready for the public came to a peak, many of us running on adrenalin. I certainly needed a lot less coffee than usual, having a natural burst of energy flowing through me. It was also not uncommon for me to survive on the occasional chocolate bar and a snatched mouthful of sandwich here and there, so big exhibition launches and events back at Charleton House often resulted in me losing a few pounds. Another reason to enjoy them!

Chelsea had done a fantastic job of mentoring the new staff through the running of the café and the high level of customer service we expected, and we had a mouth-watering display of freshly baked cakes and biscuits. We had made good use of the coffee machine over the last few days, so knew that wasn't going to let us down. Fresh sandwiches and salads were being prepared in the basement kitchen and the sun was already warming our open air courtyard.

Mark's moustache was freshly waxed and curled. He wore a wonderful tailor-made waistcoat that had a thin lime check woven through it, the back a luscious lime silk. The shop was, as you'd imagine with Joyce at the helm, shipshape. The surfaces had been dusted multiple times, and the stock was displayed like works of art. Joyce wore a rather smart pale blue suit, the skirt tight enough to show an impressive visible panty line, and the amount of chunky gold jewellery that hung from her neck and wrists and glinted off almost every finger made her look like a rather unusual rap artist. Each nail also had a little diamond glued on. The combination of her heels and the neat tower of blonde hair left her dominating the space. When one of Joyce's tills decided to stop working briefly, although an IT specialist was on the end of the phone, I'm convinced that it was the rather terrifying glare that she gave the machine which had the desired effect.

The morning went smoothly, the visitors suitably impressed by the art collection and the decorative rooms they had been displayed in. On the rare occasion I made my way into the exhibition rooms, I heard Mark capturing the imagination of groups of people with his entertainingly informative talks. The Duke and Duchess mingled with the public, welcoming them, often much to their surprise. More than one visitor was heard to ask their friends if it was 'really them' they had just spoken to.

'It's all going rather well, don't you think?'

The Duke appeared at my shoulder as I stood watching Mark talk to a group of tourists who seemed more interested in taking photos of the objects than actually looking at them.

'We had some marvellous feedback last night, and there were

so many kind words about Ambrose. Molly here has been key to all of this.' He swept his arm out in the direction of his London PA, who had just entered the room.

'Key to what? What am I being blamed for?' she asked with a smile.

'All of this. The success of the exhibition, helping us get everything organised.'

'"Helped" is the key word there, that was all I did.'

The Duke ignored her self-deprecation. 'I must leave you ladies to it. I have a lunch date with Oliver. I really wasn't sure how much we'd see of him while we're in London, so it's been a real pleasure to have so much quality time with him, and to meet more of his friends. He's surrounded himself with some very talented, capable, ambitious young people.' He gave Molly a knowing look. 'Perhaps they'll rub off on him a little.'

He quickly turned towards the doorway, where a slim figure in jeans and pale blue shirt had just walked past. 'Oliver, in here,' he called. 'We were talking about you.'

Oliver was the spitting image of his father, extremely slim with chiselled features, but a little more classically handsome. His floppy blond fringe made me think of a schoolboy who was keen on pranks and teasing his friends.

Oliver rested a hand briefly on his father's shoulder before turning to me.

'You're Sophie,' he said confidently, offering me his hand. 'I saw you at the reception. Nice to meet you properly at last.' His movements were measured, and I got the impression of someone who liked to control the moment. Everyone and everything was expected to move at his pace – a considered pace which felt slightly engineered. But despite that, it was easy to imagine that many people found him extremely attractive, and even charming.

He held eye contact with me confidently and his handshake was firm. 'I believe we have a friend in common.' He smiled, but I couldn't tell if he knew that Adam and I had once been engaged.

'I believe so.'

He turned back to his father. 'Are you ready? I have a table booked. It was lovely to meet you, Sophie; I'll see you again, I'm sure.'

I watched as they left. Mark had shown me photos of Oliver at events where everyone had been wearing expensive-looking outfits, the finest champagne had been flowing, and there was a definite tinge of hedonism to the occasion. But he also looked as if he could stride into a bank manager's office and convince them of the need for a multi-million pound loan to fund a new business. I was torn between being utterly charmed and extremely wary, and I imagined that Oliver knew exactly what impact he had on people.

CHAPTER 16

At two o'clock, I stuck my head around the door to the shop to see if Joyce was still up for a quick trip out. Gideon Snable-Bowers was doing some part-time research and teaching at the Chelsea Physic Garden, the oldest botanic garden in London created in 1673 for apothecaries to grow plants which would be used as medicines, so that was where we were heading.

I'd only visited once in all the years I'd lived in London, but I remembered a wonderful array of edible plants, and another of medicinal plants. There were glasshouses with examples of cotton, coffee and cocoa, and a pond rockery. More importantly, I recalled that the café made one of the best coffee and walnut cakes I'd ever eaten.

Joyce was clearly taking her part in our investigation very seriously and had dressed for the occasion. After doing a quick change in the ladies' toilets, she'd appeared looking like someone who was about to head out on a shoot at Balmoral. Tight fitting cream jodhpurs were tucked into brown leather boots. The white silk blouse she'd worn with the suit was partly concealed under a tweed waistcoat, both shirt and waistcoat cut as low as possible.

Her earrings were sweet little silver pheasants and much of her bling had gone. She did look rather impressive, only needing a shotgun and a flat cap to complete the image. It would be easy to think she'd look slightly ludicrous in central London, but there were plenty of stinking rich women in areas like Mayfair and Chelsea who would dress in a similar fashion to drop little Tarquin off at his private school in an SUV designed for muddy single-track lanes in the countryside. Overall, it made me wish I'd made a bit more of an effort.

THE EARL OF BAXWORTH was sitting on a low stone wall making notes when I spotted him. He looked up as we walked over and I could have sworn he did a double take as he took in Joyce. He immediately stood, which was a little unfortunate as he only came up to Joyce's nose, but he seemed at home in his surroundings. His stained cargo pants and faded polo shirt bore all the signs of someone who worked hard outdoors.

He smiled warmly at us. 'Good afternoon, ladies, you look like you might need some assistance.'

'We met the other night, Lord Baxworth. I'm Sophie Lockwood; I work for the Duke of Ravensbury, and this is Joyce Brocklehurst, one of my colleagues.'

'Ah yes, and please call me Gideon. I thought you looked familiar. You were there the night that Ambrose...' He paused, struggling to find the words, so I chose to make it easy for him.

'I was. It's shocking what happened.'

'I don't remember meeting you, though, and I'm sure I would.' He was taking in every inch of Joyce.

'I didn't work late that night, but I am interested in what happened. Can we ask you some questions?' It was framed as a request, but it was clear that Joyce wasn't giving him any options. 'Do you mind if we sit?'

Gideon indicated towards the wall and the three of us perched along the edge.

'What would you like to know? And can I ask why you're interested?' He didn't sound at all guarded, just curious.

'We realise that it's important for the Duke to understand what happened to his friend, so we'd like to find out more about it all. The Fitzwilliam-Scotts have worked very hard towards this exhibition at Ravensbury House and we really don't want the question over Dr Pitkin's death to overshadow it; the Duke and Duchess would rather people focused on his incredible research and everything he achieved over the years, rather than his untimely demise.' I was never entirely sure how to answer the 'Why are you interested?' question, but this time I rather impressed myself.

Gideon nodded. 'What would you like to know?'

'You work in the same field, don't you? Was he working on anything contentious?'

Gideon smiled at me. 'Botany is an enormous subject area, and no, we weren't working on similar subjects. Our paths crossed at events from time to time, but he wasn't someone I knew socially or ever worked with professionally. As for his work, it depends how you define contentious. He wasn't making a great impact with ground-breaking research; he was what you might consider a bit of a slogger, head down, got on with the job. He's reasonably well regarded – he'd have to be to work at the Natural History Museum – but he wasn't going to set the world on fire.'

'And what about your relationship with him? I believe you didn't get on because of his work around Caroline, the Duke's great-great-aunt.'

He took a moment to glance at Joyce, who was doing a good job of looking fascinated by every word he said.

'We got on fine. He knew how I felt about all of that, and he also knew there wasn't much I could do about it.'

'Why's that?' asked Joyce. Gideon sighed.

'I don't have hard evidence. The story about Caroline and my great-grandfather has been passed down through the family. I have no reason not to believe it, and it makes me furious that Ambrose wouldn't even consider my ancestor being the true discoverer of some rather significant plants. But I can't do much about it, and I certainly wasn't inclined to kill Ambrose over it, which is where I guess you are heading with this.'

I wasn't sure where to go next, but Joyce came to my rescue in her usual forthright style.

'Do you own a hoodie?'

'A what? Oh, one of those sweatshirts with a hood that the young people wear? No, of course not. Why would I?'

I chimed in again. 'I know you didn't work with Dr Pitkin, but did you have any sense of his reputation? Had he ever done anything to anger people, give someone a reason to kill him?'

Gideon thought for a moment before answering. 'Ambrose was a stickler for the facts. I know a couple of PhD students who worked for him and he made sure they double, even triple checked their work. That's entirely appropriate, of course, but he was quite fervent about it. It was an obsession.'

'I'd expect that amongst scientists.'

'Yes, as you should, but we don't go on about it all the time, not in the way he did. It's like he was on a mission, one that wasn't quite as necessary as he made out. If there had been failings amongst the students, then it would be understandable, but he was surrounded by very bright, conscientious people. I know it could get quite irritating. But it's not enough to make someone want to kill him. I can't imagine so, at any rate.'

'What route did you take home on Tuesday night?' Joyce's lack of subtlety was impressive.

His welcoming smile slipped behind a cloud. 'Are you suggesting I...'

'I'm wondering if you might have seen something that you

remembered after you spoke to the police. I'm not suggesting you killed him.'

'Good, I hope not. I walked up to Piccadilly, and then hailed a cab. I didn't see him after I walked out of the door of Ravensbury House.'

I couldn't think of anything else, so I stood up. Joyce and Gideon followed suit.

'Thank you for your time, Gideon.' We shook hands and his smile returned.

'I'm not sure what you think you might find, but good luck. I didn't always see eye to eye with Ambrose, but he didn't deserve this.'

As we neared the exit to the gardens, Joyce asked me to wait a moment, and then she walked back to Gideon. I wondered what she was up to.

'Are you going to tell me what that was about?' I demanded when she returned.

'He didn't have any way to contact us if he thought of anything else, so I gave him my card. I explained he could call me day or night.'

She was amazing.

'You do recall that he's penniless? He's not going to be able to whisk you off on a weekend in Monaco or take you skiing in Zermatt.'

'No, but I'm sure he can afford to take me for a drink, and after he's had a few, he might tell me anything he neglected to mention today.'

'Do you think he's keeping something from us? I thought he came across as quite genuine.'

'I really don't know, but there's no harm in double checking, and it would give me the chance to cross off one of those cocktail bars on my list.'

Wearing a smug expression, she climbed into the back of the black cab I'd flagged down. Maybe we *should* start calling her Joyce Bond.

CHAPTER 17

By the time we closed the doors of Ravensbury House at six o'clock, we could confidently declare it to have been a successful first day, and we all felt ready for tomorrow when the house was bound to be busy. Mark was insistent that we let him choose the pub we'd go to for an after-work drink and I was happy for him to lead the way on foot. Joyce said she'd get a taxi and meet us there.

I couldn't help but smile as we walked from Trafalgar Square towards the Thames; I knew where he was taking us. The Sherlock Holmes pub is popular with tourists, not just because of its name, but because it is the epitome of a London boozer. The sign swinging gently in a light breeze shows the eminent detective pondering his latest case with a pipe in his mouth, the name written across the pub's front in gold against a backdrop of black paint. Inside, a large collection of Sherlock memorabilia is on display, and episodes of old TV adaptations play on a loop on screens in each corner. It is cheesy, but an amusing choice, and the food is pretty good. Mind you, I wasn't sure what Joyce would make of the place.

We lurked until a table became free next to the door so we could get some of the evening's breeze, and claimed our spot. After I'd filled Mark in on our conversation with Gideon, he told me what he'd been able to do since I'd set him his research task yesterday afternoon.

'I've nothing to reveal yet. I have one of the curators back at Charleton House digging out any diaries from the time. Caroline wrote to her brother when she was away, so the chances are there might be something of interest in there. I also called Zannah like you suggested and I'm heading to the Natural History Museum tomorrow morning. My first tour isn't until eleven o'clock, so if I go early, I'll have time to get a general idea of what they might have in the Botany Department library. I'll have to put in a request for any historical documents, but I can do that while I'm there. If need be, I can make a trip to the National Archives at Kew, but I'll see how I get on.

'Now, you know how much I love this sort of thing, but it doesn't sound to me like Gideon is the strongest of suspects. Is it really worthwhile?'

'I'm not sure, but Gideon was there the night Dr Pitkin was killed and his family's diminished position within society probably causes him a lot of frustration and anger. It could be that there is evidence that proves his view, but he's not telling us because it would make him a suspect. If he's being honest and there isn't any evidence, then it weakens the case against him.'

'But, he doesn't own a hoodie,' Joyce chimed in, arriving by my side. 'What house of horrors have you brought me to, Mark Boxer? There's a rather hideous mounted head over there which I can only assume is meant to be the Hound of the Baskervilles. It's a good job you're married, you'd be useless at charming anyone with your choice of drinking establishment.'

'Then it's lucky you're not my type. What do you want to drink?'

'See if they have sparkling wine that looks halfway decent, otherwise I'll join Sophie in a gin and tonic. And make sure the glasses are clean.'

'What were you saying about the hoodie?' I asked.

'He said he doesn't own one.'

'I know, but are we really going to believe him just like that?'

'No, but I'm sure he's bigger than the figure in that photo the police showed us.'

'It was hard to tell how tall they were...'

'No, not that way.' She patted her stomach.

'Maybe, but a hoodie can be really deceptive, and the photo was partially over the shoulder of the mystery person, looking more towards Dr Pitkin, so we can't be 100% sure.'

'True, but I might be in a position to be a little more sure by the end of this evening. I received a text message from the Earl asking me for a drink later.'

Mark placed a glass of something pink and fizzy in front of her and a gin and tonic on the table for me. It was nothing special, but I knew we weren't here for the quality of the drinks.

'He's a fast worker,' he said. 'Have you told him where he's taking you?'

'I have indeed, the American Bar at the Savoy.'

'And you think his wallet can handle that?'

'There was a slight pause after I said that was where I'd meet him, but he agreed.'

'I can't help but feel sorry for the guy.' Mark returned to the bar for his drink, so he was unable to hear her response, which was suitable for adult ears only.

'See if he can give you any names of other people who might have had a grudge against Dr Pitkin,' I suggested.

'Don't worry, my dear, I shall charm every ounce of useful information out of him. You know, I rather enjoy helping you with these things and I've proven invaluable in the past.'

'As have I,' insisted Mark as he sat back down. 'You must feel right at home, Sophie,' he added, looking around the room between mouthfuls of beer, the usual layer of foam appearing on his moustache. 'Although I do think you're actually more of a Miss Marple, even if she does lack a fabulous hat.'

'Why am I more of a Miss Marple? I've got plenty of grey hair, but I'm not ancient.'

'Plenty of grey hair?' Mark raised a single eyebrow at me before continuing. 'Sherlock is much more cerebral, he works on an intellectual level.'

I nearly spat my drink out. 'And I'm not intellectual, is that what you're saying?'

'Umm, well, kind of. Not exactly. Sherlock is all science and logical deduction: mud on a trouser hem; a slight sprinkle of pipe ash on the collar of a jacket that most people wouldn't even see. Miss Marple is more about people, relationships, conversation. That's what you do. You're good at picking up things about people, their personalities and their inconsistencies. Sherlock gets out a magnifying glass, you and Miss Marple like the bigger picture.'

'I have no idea if any of that is true, but he does sound quite impressive. Although if I were you, Sophie, I wouldn't forget that he's basically said you are less of the little grey cells and more of the little grey hair follicles.'

'Thank you, Joyce, for the first part of that statement. Not so much for the second. Sophie knows that's not what I'm saying.'

'Actually, I think it is, but I won't take offence. You've said worse about me. I don't think you're entirely wrong, although I do prefer the deerstalker to an old woman's hat and handbag. Not that any of that helps the current situation. Hopefully I'll have a few more ideas after I've spent some time with Dr Orne at the museum tomorrow morning.'

'Just look after yourself,' said Mark with a dramatic squint. 'If he shows signs of opening any letters with something sharp, run.'

'You're an idiot, Mark Boxer.' Joyce shook her head. 'Now

you've brought me here, I assume you are buying my dinner. I'll have the most expensive thing on the menu.'

AFTER A PORTION of fish and chips that couldn't hold a candle to those I ate on a regular basis at the Black Swan in the Charleton House grounds, Mark and I said goodbye to Joyce and made her promise to remember every word Gideon said. We had decided to enjoy the warm summer evening and walked towards Ravensbury House, continuing on to Green Park Station where I would start my journey home, and Mark would keep walking to the far side of Hyde Park and the serviced apartment he was staying in.

As we walked through Trafalgar Square, Mark couldn't resist a joke about the size of Nelson's Column. We then strolled down Pall Mall and past the gentlemen's clubs, at least one of which – The Gilmore Club – the Duke was a member of. I had no idea which one was which, but they all looked like the kind of places designed to intimidate those who hadn't grown up with personal fortunes, or who didn't run banks or own vast numbers of properties around the world. I imagined that they had grudgingly permitted women as guests once they had no choice. It was another world, one I was faintly curious about, but had no desire to become a part of. Apart from anything, for all their grandeur, I would put money on their coffee being dreadful!

Any curiosity I had about which club the Duke belonged to was satisfied when I spotted a familiar face on the pavement opposite and up ahead. I grabbed Mark's arm.

'Stop, look.'

'At what, precisely?'

'Over there, isn't that Oliver? God, I hope that's not Adam with him.'

Mark peered across the road. 'Maybe, if he'd just turn... yes, yes, it is Oliver. He must have been to Daddy's club, but the other bloke doesn't look like Adam.'

He was right, it wasn't. 'Who is he?'

'No idea.'

The two men had been chatting, but now shook hands rather formally. They certainly didn't look like good friends. Oliver walked away from us, towards Ravensbury House, and the other man strode in our direction.

'What do you think that was about?' I asked. Mark turned and gave me a look of exasperation.

'I love a bit of drama as much as you, more so if truth be told, but Oliver lives here in London, and that's his father's club, so chances are he has some kind of membership as well. It was probably a meeting about another of his failed business ideas, a get-rich-quick scheme that will mean he can avoid any hard work and spend as much time as possible at the side of a pool in Monte Carlo.'

'You really don't like him, do you?'

'Not especially. He has all the trappings of the aristocracy. His parents, although they're as blue-blooded as they come, are reasonable people, and yet he still wastes every opportunity that comes his way. He takes spoilt and arrogant to a whole new level. He needs to grow up.'

'Don't hold back, now, will you?'

Mark laughed. 'I can't help it, he irritates me.'

We carried on our way, leaving the exclusive clubs to the shadows of the evening.

ZANNAH WAS out with friends when I arrived back at her flat, so I took the opportunity for an early night and climbed into bed with a book. Penny stretched along the top of my legs, adding extra heat that I really didn't need. Mark sent me a photograph of him wearing a black silk face mask with the words *sweet dreams* stitched on it in silver thread, so I knew he was home safe. I had yet to get any message from Joyce, so I assumed she was having a good night with the unsuspecting Earl of Baxworth.

It wasn't long until the book fell out of my hands as I nodded off, succumbing to my own sweet dreams.

CHAPTER 18

Entering the herbarium at the Natural History Museum was like stepping back in time. Dark wooden cabinets lined the walls, each containing rows of small narrow doors, some of which were open and I could see that they held thousands of sheets of paper. Bookcases created alcoves which held desks. Some were empty; others had been claimed by piles of books, a lamp, notebooks, a jacket left on the back of a chair.

The furniture reminded me of the staff room at my old school, all of it out of date. The worn leather on the chairs was burgundy red or dark green. There was a musty smell in the air, but it wasn't bad; it made me think of history, stories and people.

Dr Orne had met me at the door as I arrived, dressed casually in jeans and a t-shirt with a hole on the shoulder. A pair of well-worn trainers completed the look, attractive in a scruffy artist kind of way.

He saw me take in his outfit. 'Sorry, I never make much of an effort on the weekend unless I know I'm giving a talk. It's a bit like taking off my Head of Department hat and just being a scientist again. Otherwise, I feel like I never get a break.'

He was watching me as I scanned the room.

'A lot of work is done on computers now; we're currently digitising the whole collection. But there's nothing like the original specimens, the feel of them, the smell of the paper. Come with me, I want to show you something.'

He walked over to a long table that dominated the centre of the room. 'I pulled this out to show you.'

'This' was a large leather-bound green book which looked extremely old and heavy. Its pages, which had turned brown, were crinkled and had the look of paper that had got wet, and then dried imperfectly.

Dr Orne opened the book to a black and white illustration of a plant with large leaves and what looked like enormous seed pods or beans. On the opposite page were, I assumed, some of the actual leaves, dried and attached into the book. A beautiful copperplate script recorded what I guessed was the scientific name of the plant and some dates.

'This is a cocoa plant brought back from Jamaica by Hans Sloane in 1698. When he was over there, he was introduced to a drink made from this cocoa plant. He thought it was awful, but if he added milk, it became much more palatable. He brought the recipe back with him and it was initially sold as medicine. In the 19th century, a company called Cadbury's took his recipe and created chocolate.

'The idea of drinking hot chocolate became more popular because Sloane was the doctor to a queen and two kings, all of whom were encouraged to drink it. William III even had a chocolate kitchen made at Hampton Court Palace so his own chocolatier could make him hot chocolate every morning. Of course, that brought it to the attention of the general population, and look at chocolate today.

'This in front of us is called the type specimen, so it's the actual example that the naming and identification of all plants related to it are based on. It's the original that you have to refer to in order to ensure you are identifying other plants correctly, so it's the foundation. The first in the family that scientists named and described, so to speak. Not bad, eh?'

He grinned. I felt as though my eyes were sticking out of my head on stalks. It was more than not bad; it was mind-bending, thinking that this specimen had a link to every bar of chocolate on every shelf. Perhaps not genetically, but I was looking at the origin of that product, that story. I started to wonder what else was hidden away in the drawers and cupboards of the Natural History Museum, but there was a risk my brain would explode so I left that thought alone. Besides which, my reason for being here this morning, abandoning the café in the process, wasn't to admire specimens, even if that was what I wanted Dr Orne to think.

He led me through the herbarium, pointing out a few things on the way. Once we were back at his desk, I decided it was time to get stuck in.

'Dr Pitkin's death must have been a great shock to the department.'

'It was. It feels like he's off on holiday, or away at a conference. I've sent him a number of emails this week, before remembering that he won't ever receive them.'

'Was he popular amongst his colleagues?'

'He was. He got on with the job, helped people when they needed it, enjoyed the opportunity to work with the public. He organised a couple of garden parties every summer at his home, and was happy to go to the pub after work. The White Lion down the road; it does a fantastic toad-in-the-hole if you like that sort of thing. Despite all of that, he was actually difficult to get close to and could be a little intense, but that was part of what made him so good.'

'I did hear that he could be a bit obsessive, that some people struggled with that.'

'Ha, yes. He certainly wasn't one for cutting corners, that's for sure. But that's precisely as it should be in our line of work. We're all about facts, evidence.'

'Could he take it too far? Did you ever have to talk to him, as his manager, about letting some things go?'

Dr Orne seemed to give my question more thought than anything else I'd asked. He didn't look quite as relaxed as he had a moment ago.

'What have you heard?'

I shook my head. 'Nothing.'

'You seem very interested in him.'

'I am. I only met him briefly, but I really liked him; he was so passionate about his subject and I wish I could have spent more time with him. He was killed only hours after I was with him and I still think about that.' That was a slightly more impassioned version of the truth, but I needed Dr Orne to think my curiosity was nothing more than that. For the time being, anyway.

'He was a valuable member of the team and he had a lot of knowledge to pass on.'

'I was wondering; you said he could be rather intense. Did that extend to his interest in Caroline Annabelle Fitzwilliam-Scott, or the case involving Roger Ferguson?'

Dr Orne started at my mention of Ferguson. 'How did you know about that? Not that it's top secret, it's just rather obscure.'

'I stumbled across it as I did an internet search on Dr Pitkin before I came down to London. The Duke had mentioned his name and I like to know a bit more about the exhibitions we are putting on. Even though my team and I work in the café, we get all sorts of questions from the visitors.'

I didn't want to get Tess into any trouble. Fortunately, he seemed to accept my answer.

'In that case, he was very interested, yes. He felt an injustice had been done and he didn't like the idea of our work being tarnished by the actions of another.'

'And was it? Tarnished, I mean.'

Dr Orne laughed. 'Not in the slightest. It's a very old story that hardly anyone remembers. It gets referenced from time to time, but it's largely been assigned to the annals of history.'

'Why was it not dealt with more thoroughly at the time?'

'Some felt it was a storm in a teacup, others wanted to leave it until Ferguson had died. Some of his family members were botanists too and no one wanted to unnecessarily harm their reputation when they had never been involved. The other question was who had actually been harmed? He hadn't broken any rules, other than a commitment to thorough scientific research, and no one was responsible for monitoring that. His conclusions could be removed from books and reports over time. A full-blown investigation which exposed his actions would have done harm to the whole profession. As I say, he is now largely forgotten, so those who simply wanted to hush it up were right.'

'Only Dr Pitkin wanted things done properly and wouldn't let go once he got his teeth into it?'

'Correct.' By now, Dr Orne had stretched out and was looking relaxed. If any of my questions concerned him, he was doing a great job of concealing it.

'You said some of Ferguson's family were botanists.'

'Yes, his son. There might have been others, I'm not sure.'

'Is his son still alive?'

Dr Orne shook his head. 'Died last year. I remember because someone mentioned it in passing, and Ambrose overheard and started a lecture about how Ferguson was never dealt with properly. A couple of us rolled our eyes at each other and Ambrose saw. He was rather offended.'

I spotted the time on a clock on the wall. It was close to lunchtime; I had already left Chelsea alone for too long.

'Just one more thing. You and Dr Pitkin were seen arguing as you left the museum on Tuesday night; I presume you were on your way to meet the Duke for dinner. Was that about work as well?'

There was a flash of anger across his face, but he quickly got control of it.

'It was. We'd been talking about the department's budgets and why I had allocated money for a particular project. Ambrose disagreed.'

'But you were angry enough to walk off.'

The anger reappeared. 'Who saw all of this? I don't see what…' He took a breath. 'I do have some work to do and I need to get on so I can enjoy the rest of my weekend, so if you don't mind.' He narrowed his eyes and stared at me just as I was kicking myself for letting my investigative nature get the better of me. 'Is this the sort of thing the visitors to Ravensbury House are likely to ask about? Or perhaps you'd have discussed the row with Ambrose had he lived? I think not. So what's this barrage of questions really about?'

'Oh, nothing, really,' I replied, thinking quickly. 'You must excuse me, I am so nosy, I don't know when to stop sometimes. Everyone teases me for it, calls me Miss Marple. Without the bonnet, of course—'

I clamped my mouth shut, a popular expression about ceasing to dig when you find yourself in a hole springing to the front of my mind. Luckily, Dr Orne's face relaxed into a smile.

'Oh, I don't know, a bonnet could look quite fetching,' he said, laughter in his voice. I sighed with relief inwardly, but I wasn't going to get anything more out of Dr Orne now I'd pushed his buttons.

He'd strengthened the picture of Dr Pitkin as a principled and determined man. It was easy to imagine the qualities that Dr Pitkin possessed pushing someone too far and getting him into trouble; I just didn't know who it was he'd pushed. But one thing I did know: Dr Orne clearly had something to hide.

I thanked him for his time. It had been a genuine pleasure to visit the herbarium and I couldn't wait to tell Zannah what I thought. He held the door open for me and I stepped back into the main hall of the museum.

As we said our goodbyes, a familiar face came up the ornate stairs: Tess. She greeted Dr Orne and thanked him as he continued to hold the door open for her, then said a polite hello to me. Twigging immediately that she'd rather keep our meeting at Borough Market a secret, I returned her greeting as if we were strangers, then turned back to Dr Orne.

'Do many of you work on weekends?' I asked him.

'Sometimes. It's nice and quiet without the phones ringing or emails appearing every minute, a good time to get your head down and concentrate. Tess is helping me pull together some research for a conference I'm speaking at next month. This was the only way we could find the time to do it.'

They smiled at one another and I left them to it.

Tess's wasn't the only familiar face at the museum. As I passed a giant slice of a 1,300-year-old tree, wound my way down wide stone stairs, nodded politely to Darwin's statue and walked out of the main entrance, two men were just arriving, looking rather warm and out of place in their suits. When he spotted me, Detective Inspector Grey's dour expression turned into one of stony annoyance.

'Sophie Lockwood! I'm surprised you have the day off. If my memory serves me right, you've already made one visit to see the dinosaurs, and does the Ravensbury House exhibition not officially open today?' DI Grey managed to sound completely disinterested, his flat voice as colourless as his name, but I doubted that was the case. I imagined it was a persona carefully cultivated to lull people into saying more than they wanted, convincing them that it wasn't of any interest to him. Right now, he was probably running through dozens of reasons why I might be at the Natural History Museum when, as he quite rightly said, I should be somewhere else.

I decided honesty was the best policy. 'I had the opportunity for a behind-the-scenes tour and my employers kindly agreed it was not to be missed. I have a very capable café supervisor, but I'm returning now.'

'Who gave you the tour?' As the DI dug for more information, DS Knapp turned his attention to a woman who was struggling up the steps with a child's buggy. He took hold of the front and helped her to the door.

'Dr Caleb Orne, the Head of the Botany Department.'

'I know who he is.'

We stood in uncomfortable silence as overexcited children laughed and skipped their way into the building. I briefly wondered if this was going to turn into a bizarre game of chicken, but eventually DI Grey seemed to have decided he was done with me and stepped past, DS Knapp close on his heels. A goodbye might have been nice, but perhaps he was having a bad day. More likely every day was a bad day for him.

CHAPTER 19

I had been right to assume that Chelsea could cope at the café on her own, but I still felt guilty when I walked in to a long queue of people buying sandwiches, smoothies and iced coffees on the hot day. I threw myself into my work and spent the next couple of hours trying to be the model manager.

I caught the occasional glimpse of Joyce zipping around the gift shop. I doubted that she had taken any break at all, and yet she looked utterly composed, her makeup as flawless as if she had only just put it on. Mind you, she wore quite a lot, so it was probably like concrete and she'd need to chip it off with a chisel later. Mark waved at me just after lunch, but that was the only time I saw him until the very end of the day. I didn't stop running around until about four o'clock when my guilt could be damned, I needed a coffee and a very large sticky bun.

I grabbed two of each and sidled up to Joyce in the shop.

'Come on, you can take fifteen minutes.'

She glanced at the bag I was holding. 'That better contain nothing but sugar. I've burned off enough calories today that I could eat most of your cake display and I still wouldn't be back where I started this morning.'

I grinned and she followed me to the street outside. I watched with incredulity as her painted talons speared a bun, which she then proceeded to inhale; I made a start on mine before it became her next victim.

'What?' she asked as I stared. 'I've been working non-stop while *someone* had a VIP guided tour at the museum this morning.'

'Oh don't, I feel bad enough as it is.'

'I'm joking and you know it. I just hope it was worthwhile. I have to say, your Chelsea is quite the tornado. If you ever get tired of her, she can come and run the shops with me.' Joyce wasn't known for dishing out compliments readily; in fact, she'd probably ask Marie Curie why she'd only won two Nobel Prizes and what she had been doing with the rest of her time. I made a mental note to pass on the rare praise to Chelsea and get her to swear never to leave me.

'So, are you going to tell me how your date went? Will you become a countess anytime soon?'

'The American Bar really is quite something, the cocktails are divine. I had a particularly fabulous French 75; it wasn't too sweet, which is often the case.'

'And your date? I guess he didn't make that much of an impression.'

'Oh, he was alright. Perfectly nice chap, not really my type.'

'Did you learn anything useful?'

'Not especially, but why don't we go out for dinner once we've finished here? I can tell you all about it and you can tell me about your morning.'

'I have a better idea. Zannah and I were planning a girls' night in with pizza and champagne. Why don't you join us?'

Joyce seemed to consider the offer in great depth. 'Will I need to wear pyjamas with a ridiculous pattern and slippers in the shape of animals?'

'What are you…? It's not a sleepover for a bunch of thirteen-year-olds. It's me and Zannah and you can wear what you want.'

'Then I'm in. I'll get a taxi over. I expect it to be decent champagne, no fizzy rubbish from a corner shop. In fact, why don't I bring the champagne? That way I'll know it will be perfectly acceptable. You girls supply the pizza.'

'Do I need to buy some sort of low-calorie gourmet pizza from Fortnum & Mason?'

'Heavens no, pizza should be slathered with calories and served out of a cardboard box.' She took in the expression of shock on my face. 'I do know how to let my hair down; just make sure you have barbecue sauce and an extra-large tub of mint-choc-chip ice cream. The opening day of any exhibition is one of the few times I allow myself to slum it, so make it worth my while. Talking of slumming it, will Mark be joining us? I know you said it was a girls' night, but he qualifies. Almost.'

I laughed, despite the rudeness of her final comment.

'He's going to the opera, so I don't have to listen to one of your verbal tennis matches all night.'

'Oh well, more champagne for me, then. Marvellous.'

JOYCE ARRIVED at the same time as the pizza. I opened the door to find a very nervous young man holding two enormous pizza boxes, clearly intimidated by the towering specimen in killer heels with a pile of blonde hair standing rather too close to him. As I thanked him and gave him a tip, I caught her eyes wandering.

Once he was safely out of the garden gate, I stood by to let her in.

'Joyce, you terrified him.'

'What? How? He should have been flattered by my attentions.

Did you see the way those jeans fitted him? He had a remarkably tight pair of...'

'JOYCE! Behave yourself.'

She kicked off her heels and spread herself out across the cushions on the sofa like a reclining Cleopatra – if Cleopatra had worn peach-coloured jogging pants and an ocean-green t-shirt that matched the colour of her shoes. It seemed PJs were out, but loungewear was in. I passed her a couple of slices of pizza; there was no way she was moving off that sofa now she was settled. Penny slunk into the room and decided once again that Joyce's shoes looked like an easy snack.

'Sophie was telling me you had a date last night, at the Savoy,' said Zannah, handing Joyce a glass of champagne. 'Very fancy.'

'It was indeed. A rather sultry place; I wouldn't have been surprised if Frank Sinatra had walked in. Handsome young men behind the bar in white jackets, a pianist in the corner. It was like a movie set.'

'You were there with an earl – that must have made it even more dramatic.'

'I'm guessing Sophie hasn't told you much about the Earl of Baxworth. The only drama was whether or not his card was going to be declined when he paid for our drinks. I felt rather sorry for him. I don't think he was aware of how much I know about his financial situation, but I could have sworn I saw beads of sweat appear on his forehead as he passed his card over.'

'You said you didn't find out anything of use?' I prompted her, waiting as she took a drink and savoured the liquid.

'Correct. He's certainly very loyal to his family's legacy and determined to build it back up. He has all sorts of get-rich-quick schemes, few of which I imagine will see the light of day. He wants to buy back some of the land and houses that his family lost, and in the process raise their reputation to the ranks of our own dear Duke and Duchess. He even has some hare-brained idea that one of his ancestors wrote Shakespeare's plays.'

'What about the botany? Does that link him to Dr Pitkin in any way, other than their disagreement over Caroline?'

'Not that I could discover. I think he would rather like the whole plant thing to be a hobby. He certainly seems to be a clever man in regards to all of that; the business side of things, not so much.'

It was all very disappointing. I had been hoping we'd find out something useful early on, something that we could pursue to a murky conclusion to wave under the noses of the detectives, directing one to a manicurist in the process.

'What about his personality? Did he seem like the sort of person who could be involved in murder?' I asked.

'Sophie, I'm not sure *"he comes across like he could be a killer if he got annoyed"* is the best reason to point a finger at someone. No, he didn't. Obsessive, yes. He could get quite a zealous look in his eyes when he talked about some things, especially getting his family's land back, but no, I didn't think I was sharing a drink with a murderer.'

'So he's like Dr Pitkin, then,' I mused. 'Extremely passionate about things. That alone could cause a big row: two passionate men, neither prepared to back down.'

'Honestly, Sophie, I think you're wasting your time with the Earl.' Joyce passed me her empty glass. She was done talking about her date. I took the hint.

'How well did you know Dr Pitkin? Is there anything else that's come to mind?' I asked Zannah.

'Nothing in particular. I thought about him earlier when I went to buy the ice cream; I'd often see him in the local shops or cafés. He only lived a couple of streets away.'

'Really? But you never went to any of his parties?'

'No, I was never invited. It was mainly people from his own department who went to those.'

'How close is *a couple of streets?*' asked Joyce as she sat up slowly.

'A five-minute walk.'

Joyce reached for her shoes. 'What are you waiting for, girls? I think it's time to familiarise ourselves with the man outside of work.'

'What are you talking about? We're not going to learn anything from outside his house; I guess it looks just like this one.' I glanced at Zannah and she nodded in agreement.

'True, but we might be able to get in the garden, spot a few things through the windows. It's still light.'

'Which also means it's light enough for someone to spot us and call the police.'

Joyce thought for a moment. 'If anyone asks, we've lost a cat and had reports that it's been seen in the garden. Three damsels in distress over a cute kitty – people will probably come and help rather than call the police.' It wasn't a bad idea.

Joyce seemed momentarily confused as the strap on one of her shoes looked decidedly mangled and proved difficult to get through the tiny buckle; I continued to keep my mouth shut. I'd never viewed Joyce as much of an animal lover, and I didn't want to put her tolerance to any kind of serious test.

CHAPTER 20

The streets of Earlsfield were lined with Victorian terraced houses. A good number of them had been turned into flats like Zannah's; others were fashionable family homes with attics converted into extra rooms and glass extensions on the back. 'Yummy mummies' pushed baby buggies that looked so expensive, it would make your eyes water. Young professionals hung out in the nearby pubs that had been renovated and were now classed as 'trendy'. It was only eight o'clock and the heat of the day still hung in the air. Everyone we passed appeared happy and relaxed. In the warmer months, London felt like a close relation to Barcelona or Paris: a truly European city.

As we walked further away from the pubs and the high street, we passed fewer people. I could smell barbecues and hear the sound of children playing in gardens, allowed to stay up beyond their usual bedtime. Everything felt right with the world. Apart from the fact that we were on our way to sniff around a dead man's house.

. . .

ALL THE HOUSES had very small front gardens. Dr Pitkin's was so overgrown, it was almost impossible to see the front door. A tunnel had been formed by the branches of a small tree and some overgrown bamboo.

Joyce did a very obvious double take, and then darted through the gate like she was being chased by someone.

'Oh, subtle. Like that's not going to raise suspicions.'

'That ship has sailed,' called Joyce. 'I'm sure everyone round here knows he's dead, and not of natural causes. I assume it was in the papers.'

'This is London,' I pointed out as I joined her under the bushes, 'not some quaint village up north where everyone knows everyone else and you can leave your front door unlocked. Plenty of people around here have no idea who lives next door.'

'I don't know what costume drama you've been watching. I haven't left my door unlocked for years.'

'Joyce, no one would be brave enough to enter your house if you left all the doors open and put up a sign saying, "Take it, it's all yours".'

Zannah was listening with a bemused look on her face. 'Do you two actually like each other?' she asked.

'What on earth makes you think we don't?' Joyce looked genuinely confused for a moment, then returned her attention to the task in hand. 'I reckon we can get round the back through there.'

Through there was a mass of even more overgrown bushes around the side of the house. As it was the end house on a row, only one side was attached to a neighbouring property. Joyce led the way as though she was on safari and we found ourselves in a garden that was just as unkempt as the rest, but actually looked like a rather fun exotic location. More huge bamboos at the end hid the houses opposite. Large cut tree trunks had been placed around the garden and provided seating. A small fire pit looked like a lovely place to spend an evening and the overgrown grass was inviting us to sprawl out in the warmth. It was the perfect place for Dr Pitkin to host the parties for his colleagues that Tess had told us about.

'Come on,' Joyce called us over to the windows. 'There must be something of interest we can see, perhaps something else we can learn about his personality.'

I peered through the glass, wondering if what we were doing was utter madness, or if Joyce was a genius. There were some photos on the walls, but try as I might, I couldn't make out the faces in them.

I heard a rattle and looked across to see Joyce trying the back door.

'Joyce, what are you...?'

The door opened and Joyce grinned. 'It's always worth checking. Saves me breaking a window.'

'Can I help you?'

Joyce froze in position at the sound of a male voice behind us. I turned round slowly and saw, standing partway down the garden, a man with shaggy shoulder-length brown hair. He had a book in his hand and seemed to have been reading out of sight behind a clump of overgrown grasses.

Joyce turned, a look of exaggerated surprise on her face. 'I am *so* sorry. There has clearly been some kind of mistake. I'm Joyce.' She tottered down the path with an extra couple of degrees' worth of swing in her hips, and offered her hand. 'The house belongs to a friend of ours and we just wanted to check it was all secure and the garden was being taken care of. He would have hated to let it get overgrown.' She surveyed the garden as though it was proving her point.

'I know you're lying, cos if you knew my brother, then you'd know the garden was always like this and he had no intention of doing anything else with it. So, who are you really?'

I stepped forward. 'Sophie Lockwood. We – Joyce and I –

work for the Duke and Duchess of Ravensbury, and this is Zannah who works at the Natural History Museum.'

'And you're in Ambrose's garden because...?' He seemed very calm about the whole situation, but then he did have the upper hand. All he had to do was call the police and we'd be in serious trouble. Being found in the garden of a murder victim who had a connection to our employers might even cost Joyce and me our jobs. Zannah probably wouldn't fare a whole lot better, either.

'Because we want to know what happened to him.'

'Isn't that the job of the police?'

'Yes.'

The long pause that followed was uncomfortable. I couldn't get a sense of how he was likely to respond, so I was surprised when he picked up a bottle of scotch.

'Can I get you ladies a drink? I think we should talk.'

We all nodded and mumbled a few yeses and thank yous. I wasn't a big fan of whisky, but under the circumstances, I felt I should do everything I could to keep him onside.

'Grab a seat, I'll be back with some glasses.'

I couldn't resist the urge to follow him into the house, so I offered to help. 'We don't know your name.'

'Rufus.'

'And you're Dr Pitkin's brother?'

'Younger brother, yes.'

'I'm very sorry for your loss. And for, well, being here. The last thing you need now is a group of madwomen appearing in the garden.'

'True, but you've livened up a quiet Saturday night.' He passed me a couple of glass tumblers from a wooden cabinet. As we turned to leave, a row of photographs caught my eye. They were black and white shots of groups of friends in their late teens or early twenties, laughing and smiling.

'Those are from his university days. I think he put them up

when he first moved in about twenty-five years ago. If you look closely, they probably haven't been dusted since then, either.'

I looked closely. He was right. But that wasn't the only thing that caught my eye. A flash of recognition lit up my brain, then departed as quickly as it had arrived.

What is so familiar about one of those faces? I didn't have time to ponder any further; Rufus was edging towards the door, a 'let's go' expression on his face.

Back in the garden, Joyce and Zannah had made themselves at home on two of the tree stumps. Zannah looked a little nervous; Joyce looked as though it was her garden and we were her staff bringing her a drink.

'This is Rufus,' I said, rapidly bringing the others up to speed as he poured us each a drink. The measures were uneven; there was something wonderfully casual about his whole approach to life. His loose brown shorts were badly creased, his grey t-shirt had a hole in the stitching at the neck. He sat on the thick grass, looking like a man comfortable in nature. I imagined him having an allotment and his own chickens.

'Do you live here?' asked Zannah.

'No. It took the police a couple of days to track me down, but once they had, I came straight here. They told me they had finished searching the property and were fine with me moving in. I want to be here while they continue with the investigation, and then I'll need to sort out his things.' He smiled. 'I'll mow the lawn before I go, too.'

'Were you close to Dr Pitkin?' I asked.

'Please, call him Ambrose. He wouldn't have wanted any formality. To answer your question, I used to be, when we were children. Once we went to university we saw less of each other. He went to Oxford while I was up at Edinburgh, then immediately went on to do a DPhil. He'd visit our parents for occasional weekends, but they only coincided with my visits maybe once or twice a year.'

'So you hadn't seen him recently?' Joyce was pretending to drink her scotch, which I knew she hated.

'Not for a while. We spoke on the phone the other week, but it had been months before that. I really feel I should be asking some questions, like why were you about to break into my murdered brother's house?'

'When you put it like that, it does sound rather bad,' I conceded. 'We hadn't actually planned to break in; the cat burglar over there can be blamed for that.' I raised my eyebrows at Joyce, who merely raised her still full glass of scotch in response. 'But we did wonder if we might spot something that could throw some light onto your brother's murder.'

'Don't you think the police might have done that already?'

'Yes, but no one's perfect.' Joyce knocked her scotch back and her whole face screwed up in a grimace that would have won her first prize at the World Gurning Championship. She shook her head, let out a gasp of air, and then kept talking as if nothing had happened. 'There is every chance that we would have spotted something the police didn't; I'm not sure I trust those two detectives who are working on the case. They both look like they need help doing up their shoelaces.'

'And you want to find out more because?'

'I don't have a good answer for that. We met him, we liked him, it's shocking and justice needs to be done,' I said honestly.

'And they've done this kind of thing before.' It was Zannah's turn to speak. I was surprised to find she had drained her glass and was accepting the offer of a top-up from Rufus.

'You've done what before?' Rufus looked confused.

'Sophie has been involved in solving a few murder cases.'

'*We* have,' Joyce corrected, never one to be left out.

'Well, that sounds interesting, and I have to admit the police are doing a pretty poor job of keeping me up to date. I was offered a family liaison officer, but I turned them down, so I suppose it's my own fault really. But if you can speed things up and get to the bottom of this…'

I wasn't listening to him anymore as I walked back into the house and to the room with the drinks cabinet. With one of the framed black and white photographs from the wall in my hand, I returned to the garden.

'I couldn't work out what was so familiar about this photo earlier, but now I realise.' I passed the photograph to Joyce, and Zannah leaned in. 'See anyone you recognise?'

'They just look like a bunch of sickeningly happy and healthy young people who have yet to experience the harsh realities of life.' Joyce looked at me. 'What? It's the truth. You know it, I know it, we all know it. Apart from anything, one of them is going to be killed, which rather proves my point.'

'Look at the woman to the left. The blonde.'

'It's a black and white photo, how do I know… isn't that, oh, what's her name? The climber.'

'Mountaineer, Fleur Lazarus. Yes, I think it is.'

CHAPTER 21

I felt a sense of relief flood over me. Finally, I was onto something. Fleur had stated very clearly to me that she didn't know Ambrose and their paths had never crossed at university. Here was evidence that she was lying.

I looked up at Rufus. 'Was Ambrose a mountaineer?'

'He did a little when he was at uni. Our parents took us hiking all the time when we were growing up so it made sense that he kept it up, and his research took him to some interesting places. I don't think he was a particularly serious mountaineer; it quickly became all about the research and the hard-to-reach places the hiking and climbing could take him.'

'Did he ever mention the name Fleur Lazarus?'

He thought for a moment. 'Not that I can recall. Like I said, we didn't have a lot of contact.'

'Did he continue with it when he left university, the mountaineering?'

'No, at least not that I'm aware of. After he finished his first degree, I got the impression he had become a full-on science nerd. It was all about his work. Whenever we tried to get the four of us together, he'd tell Mum and Dad he was working on a project and would be in some lab or other all weekend. He did go home, just not as often as me. I started to imagine him as the lonely science professor whose only relationship was with his microscope, probably even slept in a white coat, so I was surprised to find photos of parties here in the garden while going through his things.'

I wondered whether something had happened that had made Ambrose become more sociable, or if his brother had just had the wrong picture of him all these years. 'You said you spoke to him on the phone recently. Did he seem concerned about anything? Upset?'

'No, not especially. He did say that he was worried about a friend who was making some bad choices.'

'Any idea who that was?'

'None.'

'Can I keep this?' I indicated the framed photo.

'Sure.'

Joyce and Zannah's glasses were empty, so I felt it was time to head home. I didn't want any more whisky, and although Rufus had been happy to chat, he had found us trying to break into his brother's house, and that was hardly the best start for an evening of warm and witty conversation.

Zannah seemed to read my thoughts and stood up, handing Rufus her glass as she did so. 'Thanks for the drinks, and sorry for crashing your evening like this.'

He laughed. 'You're the friendliest burglars I've ever come across, and I'm pretty sure most burglars don't have the good intentions you do.'

'Absolutely,' confirmed Joyce. 'I realise our methods are a little unorthodox, but we find that they work.' She made us sound like a full-time crime-fighting outfit that had its own TV series, but there was nothing about her peach and green outfit that was subtle enough for her to sneak around, catching the bad guys.

Rufus seemed unable to come up with a response. He was right not to try.

'If you have any more questions, you know where to find me, and I'd love to know if you discover anything.' I nodded and shook his hand, grateful that we were walking out of the garden without a police escort.

JOYCE HAD HAILED a taxi that passed us on the walk back to Zannah's, so it was just the two of us and Penny. Zannah and I finished off the slightly flat champagne and the remaining cold slices of pizza; neither of us was hungry, but we were both without any food-related willpower, so got stuck into devouring the leftovers.

'Are you going to talk to Fleur?' Zannah asked as she watched me feed Penny a lump of cheese. 'She's going to be twice the size by the time you leave.' Penny looked up at me with longing in her eyes.

'I don't think she minds that idea. Besides which, all that fur will hide her waistline. Yes, I am. She's giving one of her talks at the Royal Geographical Society tomorrow evening.' I pulled up the website on my phone. 'Do you want to come? They have tickets left. It would be a nice way to spend a Sunday evening.'

'Thanks, but I'm already busy.'

I bought my ticket and wondered what reason Fleur could have to lie about Ambrose; I assumed that she had lied to the police as well. There was, of course, the chance that she hadn't spent much time with Ambrose and it was the other people in the photo who meant something to him. Perhaps he'd had clearer, fonder memories of that time than anyone else and the other people in the photo would have to wrack their brains in order to remember him.

There were some real contradictions about his personality. He was a quiet science nerd according to his brother, while being comfortable with the public and encouraging people to engage with science according to Zannah. He hosted parties at his house, yet didn't seem to be the life and soul of the department at the museum. If anything, he frustrated his colleagues. I'd met the man and liked him, but the more I talked to other people, the more my impressions of him were getting cloudy and jumbled up.

I wanted to talk to Tess again. She had attended some of his parties and knew what kind of host he was. Perhaps there had been a guest who'd stood out or something of note she had seen.

'Does Tess work Sundays?' I asked Zannah.

'No, she's Monday to Friday only.'

I shook my head. 'She was in today, helping Dr Orne prepare for a conference.'

'Was she really?' Zannah's eyes had lit up.

'What?'

She gave a snigger. 'She kept that one quiet.'

I turned to look at Penny. 'Do you reckon she's going to tell us?' Penny gave a little squeak of a meow. 'I'll pin her down, you stick your claws in her until she talks.'

'Give over. It's just that I've always wondered if she has the hots for Caleb. She says she doesn't, that she wouldn't get involved with a married man, but she likes him, a lot, and I swear she gets a misty-eyed look whenever he comes up in conversation. Also…' She paused for effect and drained the last few drops of wine into her glass, giving it a ceremonial shake and placing it slowly on the table. I was ready to throw something at her. 'Also, a couple of my team were telling me that he's a bit of a ladies' man. He came on to one of them in the pub a while ago, and she says she's not the only one he's approached.'

'He's a good-looking man, it's not hard to imagine that a few women have fallen for his charms. Do you think it might be related?'

'To Ambrose's death? Do you mean Caleb might have tried it

on with someone Ambrose was involved with? Has there been any mention of Ambrose having a girlfriend?'

'No, but do you think you could have a sniff around at the museum? Try and find out if there was someone. It might have been someone that he shouldn't have been involved with and they had to keep it quiet.'

'You mean a married woman?'

'Possibly, or someone more senior and an affair might have compromised her position. While you're at it, try and get Tess to spill the beans. She likely won't want to drop Dr Orne in it, but she might say something without realising its significance.'

Zannah grinned at me. 'This is all rather exciting. As soon as I get into work, I'll ask Tess if she fancies going for a coffee. She's never turned me down yet.'

I settled back into the sofa and Penny climbed onto my lap, circling round a couple of times before finally getting comfortable. When she was tightly wrapped up and her face was hiding under her paws, she looked like a ginger pom-pom. She seemed to weigh nothing and my fingers sank into her fur as I stroked her.

'I think she likes me.'

'You spoil her. Stay here much longer, she'll be as fat as Pumpkin.'

I could feel Penny's chest rise and fall, and the gentle motor of her purr. I was feeling much more relaxed now I had something to go on, questions to ask and some areas of confusion to clear up, and was looking forward to tomorrow. I'd wanted to see Fleur's talk anyway, and hopefully I was going to learn about a lot more than just mountaineering.

CHAPTER 22

It was a forty-minute walk to the Royal Geographical Society, just up the road from the Natural History Museum by the corner of Hyde Park. I chose a route along a path next to Rotten Row, a sandy track within the park for people to ride their horses along. Children ran in circles round trees, some shouted at by their parents as they got too close to some rather vicious looking geese. Couples took photos of one another or lazed on the grass.

Summer in London always felt like a holiday to me, whether or not I'd been at work or was on my way there, and it felt no different now. I'd spent the day on my feet with a mild hangover, and yet I found myself with an extra spring in my step. I smiled at everyone I made eye contact with and felt as though anything and everything was possible.

I walked out of the park onto Exhibition Road and entered a single-storey modern glass building that connected to an older red-brick one. This was the Royal Geographical Society. Built at the end of the 19th century, the older building had been extended in various directions over the years.

People were standing chatting in a white foyer, others gradually making their way into a theatre and finding seats ready for Fleur's presentation. A large image of Fleur greeted the guests as they entered – or at least, I assumed it was Fleur as the figure in the image was covered head to toe in a down-filled one-piece suit, the hood pulled tightly around her face, a bright blue sky and the craggy top of a mountain reflected in her goggles, an ice pick held high in one hand.

I chose a seat halfway down the modern auditorium. This wasn't just me trying to get more information, I was genuinely interested in what Fleur had to say. I had no plans to replicate her achievements; I didn't have any desire to climb Everest or K2, and as far as I was concerned, snow was best viewed from the inside of a warm pub, a roaring log fire toasting my feet and a large plate of fish and chips in front of me. The idea of climbing to 29,000 feet and surviving on melted snow and chunks of chocolate did nothing for me. However, I enjoyed hearing other people's tales of derring-do, so I was looking forward to this.

And Fleur didn't disappoint. After a brief introduction by the Director of the Royal Geographical Society, she launched into the story of her various expeditions: the challenges the weather had thrown at her team, the lack of oxygen, the risks of frostbite. Passing the bodies of less fortunate climbers who had gone before, now frozen in place as a stark warning of the dangers ahead. The feelings of fear and exhilaration, and the disappointment of sometimes having to accept that you must turn around, the peak yet to be reached, the conditions too dangerous to continue. It was all made even more remarkable by the strength that inhabited such a slim frame. I wondered where Fleur stored the energy she required, why she hadn't snapped in the 30-plus mph winds or been blown off the mountain peaks as she was taking a celebratory selfie. She was a remarkable woman, and as her talk came to an end and she took questions from the audience, I felt a great wave of pride that I knew her.

However, I was also convinced that she had the strength, tenacity and wit to take Ambrose's life. She talked of survival and the risks she had taken, and I wondered if those risks extended to murder. But the way she talked of the celebration of life, the variety of talents that lie within us all, of overcoming differences and working together made me wonder if murder was her style. This was a woman who faced problems head on; she didn't just push them out of the way and keep going without looking back. Just how far she would go to deal with a problem was another question altogether.

AFTER FLEUR HAD RECEIVED A WELL-DESERVED, loud and lengthy round of applause, the auditorium quickly emptied, many people heading straight to the bar. From there, some moved to the warmth of the evening in an enclosed garden; others, including Fleur, remained inside. I had half wondered if I would see the Duchess here to support her friend, but as she had gone out for the day with the Duke, I guessed they were probably spending the evening together as well. She had no doubt already heard Fleur speak and learnt a great deal about her trips when the two of them had spent time together.

I watched Fleur as I ordered a gin and tonic at the bar. She was laughing loudly at comments made by an older, rather rotund gentleman. His face the colour of beetroot, his tie even from a distance screaming, 'I'm privately educated and one of the chaps', he in turn appeared to be enjoying being seen with the star of the evening. Fleur rested her hand lightly on his arm as she responded to his comments; she certainly knew how to make someone feel like the centre of attention.

The Director who had introduced her talk made his way over, introducing Fleur to a couple who had followed him. I desperately wanted to talk to her, but I was also aware that tonight would be partly about networking for Fleur, gaining the attention of people who might help finance future expeditions, so I hung back people watching, and eventually ordered a second drink.

'Let me get that.' Fleur handed a twenty-pound note to the barman as he placed a glass in front of me. 'It's the least I can do to say thank you for coming. I'll have the same.'

'Thank you, you didn't need to.'

'No, but I wanted to. You're here alone?'

'I am. I was hoping I would get a chance to talk to you, but everyone wants some time with you, understandably.'

'True, and it's exhausting. Come on, let's go outside. I could do with a break before I dive back into the fray.'

She led the way to a large rectangle of grass. A few people raised their glasses to her and shouted 'well done' or 'great talk' as she walked by. A bench on the far side had just been vacated, so we took a seat next to a bank of fragrant jasmine and honeysuckle. Closed off from the noise of the traffic, tucked away in a private garden enjoying the warm evening and the floral scents, we'd have been forgiven for not realising we were in one of the busiest cities in the world.

'So, how can I help? Would you like to head out into the wilds of Antarctica?' From the grin, I knew she was joking.

'An Arctic Roll is as close as I want to get,' I said, thinking of the childhood dessert I had been very fond of. 'I'm blown away by what you've done, but I'm happy to be an armchair adventurer. No, I wanted to talk to you about Ambrose.'

'Ah.' A serious expression replacing her previously happy one, she took a sip of her drink, and then looked down towards her feet. 'I was waiting for someone to say that to me, but I was rather expecting it to be the police. Not a café manager... no offence.'

'None taken. But if you were expecting it, then it tells me that you were waiting for someone to realise you had more to say.'

She didn't immediately look up. After what felt like an eternity, she turned to face me.

'Yes, I knew Ambrose better than I let on. But then, I guess you already knew that.'

CHAPTER 23

'Can you blame me for not letting on how well I knew him? The most likely suspects are the ones who were at Ravensbury House that evening. We knew he was there, we could have waited for him, or followed him. If I said I knew him, then the police would start looking into my background, talking to people, and I don't need that, not now. I know that sounds selfish, but I didn't do it, and disrupting my life, maybe even making sponsors pull out of my next expedition, is not going to bring Ambrose back.'

'You're right, it won't change what's happened, but it might help the police rule a few things out and focus their energy where it's needed.'

'Not if they are wasting time looking at things that aren't relevant, which is what they would be doing if they viewed me as a suspect.'

She had a point, but she still hadn't told me enough. 'So, how well did you know him? You met at university – was it at the Mountaineering Club?'

Fleur nodded. 'He was a keen hiker, but hadn't done anything more taxing than climbing Snowdonia in the summer and wanted to try something a bit more challenging. He liked the idea of travelling to exotic places and seeing interesting plants in their original setting, rather than a botanical garden in the centre of a city. Mountaineering skills would help him with that. He came on a few trips, mainly rock climbing in Scotland or France, but we did make a trip to Everest Base Camp. After about a year, he stopped coming along.'

'Do you know why?'

'No. I always assumed that he got more and more caught up in his studies. He liked a drink, went to the occasional party, but he wasn't the stereotypical student. He already knew he wanted to do a DPhil and go on to do research, so it made sense that he worked hard. He had to.'

'Did you keep in touch after university?'

She shook her head. 'I didn't talk to him again after he left the club, it was the only thing we had in common. I saw him around Oxford occasionally, outside the Bodleian, that kind of thing, but not really to talk to. I did know he was here in the capital; he was interviewed on the news for a report on the pollen count in central London and the presenter said he worked at the Natural History Museum.'

I couldn't help but notice that for a confident woman who apparently had nothing to hide, she was spending a lot of time staring at her shoes as she talked, and it was starting to make me uncomfortable. Was she still lying? Perhaps she just felt awkward about having lied, or upset about Ambrose.

'Did you know he was going to be at Ravensbury House the night he died?'

'No, I had no idea. The Duchess had said that her husband had some guests coming over later, but I didn't know who they were. There was no plan to join them; it was coincidence that I came down to leave as they were in the hall, otherwise I might never have known.'

'But why not tell this to the police? They would have had no reason to suspect you. If they find all this out later, they'll have more reason to question your motives for hiding the information.'

'I realise that, I think about it every day. I've been waiting for someone to come knocking on my door.'

'Only you expected it to be the police. I guess this is slightly better.'

'It's a relief to tell someone. I haven't spoken to anybody about it, I haven't even told my friends I was at Ravensbury House that night.'

'In case they told the police you knew Ambrose?'

She looked up quickly. 'Of course not. Anyway, I don't know anyone from my university days, not very well. We all moved on.' A cloud of concern swept across her face before being replaced with something more closely resembling the confident speaker I had seen earlier. 'I don't have anything to hide. Look, I'm glad we had this chat, honestly. But I really ought to talk to a few more of the guests. There are some important people that I want to make sure I'm introduced to. Sorry, Sophie, I have to go.'

I drained my glass and stood up. We walked back in together, and as we stood near the entrance, Fleur thanked me for coming.

She kissed me on both cheeks and then paused before saying, 'Look, I feel bad asking, but would you mind not repeating any of this to the Duchess?'

'Of course. There is no reason for it to come up. I'll just say how much I enjoyed your talk, no more.'

'Thank you, I appreciate it.' A look of relief accompanied the smile she gave me as I left.

I ALLOWED myself to wander aimlessly though the streets behind the Royal Geographical Society, thinking about my conversation with Fleur. I still admired her. It was remarkable what she had put her mind and body through in the mountains, and she wanted to do it all over again, despite knowing the risks she would face, including the ultimate risk of possibly never returning home.

I tried to push my awe aside and focus on what she had said. She had admitted very quickly to knowing Ambrose, even though she hadn't known how much I was aware of. She also didn't know about the photograph, so she could have kept lying if she'd really wanted to, unaware she was digging a hole for herself. She hadn't and that went in her favour, but something wasn't quite right. So many emotions had crossed her face during our conversation, I was sure she would be well advised never to play poker. There was something she wasn't telling me, and revealing only part of the story was likely her way of putting me off the scent. I didn't feel that she was involved in Ambrose's murder, but she hadn't been completely honest with me, and it was clear she wasn't going to be. If I pushed too hard and angered her, then she had the ear of the Duchess, and I already spent enough of my time trying to juggle my work with the digging around I was doing. I didn't want to lose the support and favour of my employers.

I decided to enjoy the evening for as long as possible before jumping on a hot and sweaty underground train. The buildings in this part of South Kensington are an imposing mixture of Edwardian and Victorian terraces, alongside a few 1970s monstrosities from when the various universities expanded. Still wondering about Fleur's claim that she hadn't seen Ambrose since university, I wasn't paying a lot of attention to where I was heading, until I was abruptly pulled back into the moment by the sound of raised voices getting ever closer.

Further down the road, by the side of a car, a couple were arguing. I couldn't make out what they were arguing about as the man kept shushing the woman, talking in lower tones. At one point, he pulled her to him and tried to keep her in an unwanted embrace. I initially thought that maybe she needed help, but it was clear she could take care of herself as she pulled away and continued ranting at him.

As I got closer, I could hear the occasional word she shouted at him. 'Promise… wasting my time… I can't believe.' I was surprised at the volume and strength of such a small woman's voice. Hovering behind a row of large plane trees, I told myself that far from just being nosy, I wanted to be able to call for help if things got ugly.

It was when the woman started to walk across the road away from the man that I recognised them both. Caleb Orne and Tess Little were, if what Zannah had said was right, in the middle of a lovers' tiff.

CHAPTER 24

The text said, '*It would be lovely to see you, and I'd really like to show you the restaurant. I think you'll be impressed.*' There was a link to an address.

I stared at my phone. After watching Tess storm off up the road, I'd meandered towards Kensington High Street station, deciding to catch the Tube from there, but I'd been stopped in my tracks by the beep of my phone and Adam's name appearing on the screen. He hadn't needed to give me the address; I'd done some online stalking after I'd seen him at the Ravensbury House reception and I knew that his restaurant was in Notting Hill. I also knew that I would visit the restaurant while I was in London, curiosity getting the better of me, but my plan was to take Mark for company.

I stood on the corner of a street, wondering what to do. It would be churlish of me not to take him up on his invitation and I was only twenty minutes' walk away. I didn't want him back in my life, not even on the periphery. I didn't have any questions to ask him; I didn't even want to know if he'd been in love with the server he'd slept with. I didn't want to know if he had been trapped into taking the money from the restaurant we had both worked for. I didn't want to know if he was keeping his nose clean and staying out of trouble. But the least I could do was say hello. I cared enough to wonder if he was happy and healthy, but only in the way I cared whether a vague acquaintance was happy and healthy.

As I considered all this, I felt a great wave of relief come rushing over me. I really was over him, over the whole sorry history. I had moved on and had a wonderful life with wonderful friends in Derbyshire. I was single, but I really didn't care. Seeing him wasn't going to cause me any pangs of regret, or make me suffer as I relived moments of pain.

With renewed energy, I strode forward into the road, and nearly got hit by a black cab. I marched on; I was going to visit Adam at his restaurant and I was going to be fine. Anyway, I'd always loved visiting restaurants when I lived here, seeing what the competition was up to, seeing what delights the chef was creating, discovering new cocktails at the bar as I waited for a seat. It would be fun, and I would expect Adam to pick up the bill.

The restaurant, *Elemental,* was in the basement of a white townhouse that at one point would have housed a very wealthy family. Despite its underground position, it was large with high ceilings. I had expected a dark jazz-club style atmosphere, but instead, plush honey-beige chairs surrounded wooden tables, all framed by white walls and very expensive looking modern paintings.

A smart bar ran along one side of the room. Another wall opened up onto the kitchen and I could see the chefs at work. I took a seat at the bar just as Adam came out of the kitchen.

'My God, Sophie, I didn't think you'd come. It's so good to see you.' I let him kiss me on the cheek, but made no move to embrace him. 'Evan, a glass of champagne for my guest, please.' He looked me up and down. 'You really do look well, the country air must agree with you.' There was a smooth tone to his voice which made him sound utterly charming without a hint of sleaze; it was one of the things that made him good at his job. Everyone felt like his special guest, and I'd yet to see him faced with an irate customer that he couldn't talk down and have eating out of the palm of his hand in no time.

'It does, I'm very happy in Derbyshire.' A glass of champagne, which perfectly matched the colour of the chairs, was placed before me, and I saw Adam indicate to the barman that he would like one too. With a glass in his hand, he raised it in a toast. He was considerably taller than me, but he had never made me feel looked down upon, like the little woman by his side. I couldn't even begin to describe how he did it.

'To you and your country bumpkin life.'

I took a sip. The champagne was very dry, cut with an apple flavour; exactly as I liked it. Looking at the bottle it had come from, I would expect it to be exquisite.

We exchanged small talk for a while, both of us avoiding the subject of his spell locked up at Her Majesty's pleasure. Whenever he tried to bring the conversation around to his indiscretion, I would change the subject. I didn't want to dwell on the past. He even tried to apologise, but I batted that away as well and hoped that would tell him I didn't need to hear 'sorry', that I had moved on.

'So how do you know Oliver Fitzwilliam-Scott?' I asked.

'He started coming in here; he used to have a flat around the corner and he'd bring friends. We got chatting and it went from there. He's a good laugh. Just one moment…' Throughout our conversation, Adam had occasionally gone to say goodbye to a customer, take questions from his staff, or check on something in the kitchen. This time, he went to talk to a group of wealthy looking young men who had occupied a large round table in the far corner. The space was designed in such a way that it could be considered a semiprivate area. I watched as Adam enquired after their food, and then engaged the man who appeared to be the host in conversation away from the rest of the group. I wondered if there was a complaint as they both looked rather serious.

A phone beeped and I reached for mine; it was blank. I then spotted Adam's, which he'd left on the bar beside me. I checked that Evan was busy making cocktails, and then moved the phone closer to me, reading the text message.

'DY says he's paid. Check the account'. It was sent from a contact called 'Oliver FS'.

I pushed the phone away from me before Adam returned. He was doing business with Oliver? Instinctively, I didn't like the sound of that.

Elemental was an incredibly classy place for an ex-con like Adam to get a job in, but then there was no escaping the fact that he was very good at his job. When we were together, he had regularly been head-hunted for restaurant manager roles around the city, so it didn't entirely surprise me that he had been able to find someone prepared to take a chance on him following his release. Although if they had any sense, they'd be keeping a close eye on the restaurant accounts.

'You know, if you wanted to come back to London, I'm sure I could put in a word...'

'Don't even think about it. I wouldn't work with you, let alone *for* you, again if you offered me all the tea in China, and I'm more than happy where I am.'

He looked momentarily hurt. 'You hate tea so I'd be surprised if you turned me down for that. I'd offer you a lot of coffee, and a decent salary.'

He'd always been too sure of himself. It was time to go.

'Sophie!'

'Linda! What are you doing here?' The server, with her dark hair tied back in a tight bun and a smile that I had seen used to calm the most belligerent and drunken customers, had worked with me before I left the city. We seemed to follow each other from restaurant to restaurant and she had been a joy to work with.

'This one convinced me to join him.' She jabbed a thumb towards Adam. 'Someone needs to look after him, and the chef has become one of the top ten to watch in London, so I thought it might be interesting.'

'She couldn't resist my charms.' Adam grinned. Linda rolled her eyes; she had the measure of him.

'I have to go, but don't be a stranger. Make sure you come and say hello again.' She smiled as she turned towards a table of four. I liked Linda and knew that she wouldn't be here for Adam; she put up with him rather than actually liking him. The chef must have been good.

The host at the table in the corner caught Adam's eye again.

'I'll be back.'

'No, hang on.' I drained my glass and stood up. 'I only came to see this place. I should be going.'

'Are you sure? I could get some food sent out to you.'

'No, thank you.'

'Okay, well, look, I have the night off on Tuesday. We could…'

'No, we couldn't, Adam. It's been good to see you and I'm glad you're getting on with life. But that's all.'

He shrugged. 'Okay, but please come back for a drink again, or dinner. Bring your friends.' He kissed me on the cheek before returning to the group.

I walked out into the summer evening, pleased I had made the effort. I didn't feel quite so pleased about the text message from Oliver; that had left me decidedly uncomfortable, and I wondered how I was going to find out more.

CHAPTER 25

My little café courtyard was a calm, bright oasis early in the day. We had a couple of hours until we opened, so Mark and I were enjoying a leisurely coffee with our feet up on the chairs. Mark was filling me in on his Saturday night visit to the Royal Opera House, his waistcoat hanging open, his shoes polished into a mirror-like state of perfection.

'It really was sublime, possibly the best *Carmen* I have ever seen. I'm considering going again, fancy joining me?'

I peered at him over my mug. I like to think of myself as reasonably cultured, but I have my limits.

'If I can take a book and some earplugs, sure. I imagine they have a well-stocked bar if the earplugs don't work.'

'You're a philistine, Sophie Lockwood. I'd be better off taking Pumpkin. Talking of which, I have a complaint to make.'

'Another one?'

'Bill sent me a photo this morning, she's taken to sleeping on my side of the bed. I told him very clearly that she must not sleep on the bed, but now she spends the night with her head on my pillow, looking for all intents and purposes like she owns the place. I'm a little worried that I'll be in the spare room when I return.'

I was always nervous when I went away, Pumpkin being my surrogate child, but now I wondered if she was even going to return to me. I wasn't going to swap her for Mark, that was for sure.

I changed the subject. 'You wanted to tell me something?'

'Yes, I spent some of yesterday afternoon on the phone with one of the curators back at Charleton House. She's doing some research and, despite it being a Sunday, was going into work anyway, so said she'd check out anything she could find on Caroline for me. The archives have a number of letters Caroline sent to her brother and at least one of her journals, but that will take longer to find. In the meantime, she photographed and sent over the relevant letters.' He waved some sheets of paper at me. 'She was quite something, our Caroline, nothing seemed to faze the old girl. Listen to this:

"It's been a challenging journey to my current destination. Over the last few weeks, I have had to deal with drunk men, robbers, a number of snakes and some extremely troublesome natives. Fleas and mosquitoes have tested my patience, and I must tell you about an encounter with a lion, but I will save that for a future letter".'

'Where was she?'

'Somewhere in Africa. The first page of the letter is missing so I'm not sure when it was written. There is one here from 1889:

"It is here that I met a Mr Jacob Snable-Bowers. We felt that remaining together for a portion of the journey might be wise to enable me to travel without suspicion. He is pleasant company, although I feel our interests differ. He is amassing a worthy collection, but beyond that, I am unsure where his curiosity lands. He shows little interest in the great additions we are making to science and our understanding of the natural world. I feel he could collect almost anything and be just as happy".'

'So he wasn't the great explorer that Gideon makes out.'

'Maybe not, but remember that Caroline had only just met him. She might have been jumping to conclusions, he might have been a bit more low-key about his interests. Either way, it was early days. She was fifty-three when she met him, which was an incredible age for a woman of her class and status to still be travelling. She defied society's expectations in so many ways and clearly loved it.

'I've only had access to ten of her letters and there are very few references to Jacob, but I have got a better picture of her. She loved being in a man's world and the freedom that travelling gave her. She was reluctant to have to travel with a man, even when it was safer to do so; it would have been a great source of frustration for her to decide to stay with Jacob for this reason.'

'And she remained single all her life?'

Mark nodded. 'She never married. There is one line in here; hang on.' He went through the papers in his hand until he found what he was looking for. '"*I am sorry if I disappoint you, my dear brother, but I have yet to come across a man who interests me as much as the treasures that nature has laid before me, one who can compete with the beauty or provide a level of conversation that I would swap my beloved solitude for. It is not a husband I seek on my journeys, and I would be most grateful if you would refrain from having a potential suitor waiting in the wings when I return to visit you. As grateful as I am for your concern, your precious time will have been wasted and the gentleman will have to return home alone*".'

'I would have got on with her!' I declared. 'Any more?'

'Not yet. I'll keep you posted.' Mark stood up and fastened the buttons on his waistcoat. 'Must dash, my audience will be arriving.'

I checked my watch. 'We have a while yet.'

'The Duchess has asked me to give a private tour. The group has some connection to one of the sponsors of the exhibition. It will either be the spoilt brats of some wealthy donor or a group of bankers who have no interest in the art, but will spend their time wondering how much the Duke and Duchess would want if they offered to buy the house in order to gut it and turn it into an exclusive club with a rooftop swimming pool.'

'Cynic.' I knew he spoke from experience, though, and he hated having to give tours to people who spent most of the time on their phones. To date, Mark had bitten his tongue, but one of these days, I was sure it would get back to me that he'd ripped a phone from the hands of an overindulged teenager and thrown it out of a window. I could only wish that I would be there to witness it if it ever happened.

I stayed in my seat and pulled up the internet on my phone, wanting to find out more about Fleur's mountaineering days as I remained convinced that she wasn't telling me everything. I searched the University of Oxford's website and eventually navigated my way to the Mountaineering Club's page.

There were dozens of photos of healthy-looking young people in beautiful areas, from snow-topped mountains to giant slabs of rock in forests. It took me a while to hunt around on the small screen; there didn't seem to be an archive of photos from over the years, but there was a list of past presidents. I looked for the years that Fleur and Ambrose would probably have been members and went through them.

Each name was accompanied by a photograph that I could click on to open up the profile. I went through a couple of them, eventually selecting a black and white photo of someone called Nicholas Fry whose face was familiar. When the profile opened up, I realised that the photo was exactly the same as the one I had taken from Ambrose's home, cropped to remove the other people in the image.

Nicholas Fry had been the president of the Oxford University Mountaineering Club, and he had spent time with Ambrose and Fleur. It didn't take a lot of searching to discover that he had gone on to medical school and now worked as a GP in Surrey.

His practice was a thirty-five-minute train ride from central London.

I knew what I would be doing tomorrow. There had to be more to Fleur's association with Ambrose, and I hoped that Dr Fry could help me find out what it was.

WE WEREN'T AS busy in the café as we had been at the weekend, but I still only stepped out from behind the counter to clear tables or fetch more food from the kitchens, so was kept fully distracted from thoughts of the murder. Today, we were serving a roasted pepper and goats' cheese sandwich, the cheese coming from a farm on the Charleton House estate, and a ploughman's lunch that included a chutney the Duchess had helped create. It was these little touches that made visitors feel closer to the Duke and Duchess and their lives which went down a storm, especially with our older customers.

At about three o'clock, Molly dropped in. 'The Duke is taking the train back to Derbyshire – just an overnight visit, he'll be back late tomorrow. Would you mind putting together a takeout meal he could have for dinner on the train? A sandwich would be fine, he says he doesn't mind what.'

I gathered together a beef and horseradish sandwich, remembering that it was his favourite filling, and a scone freshly baked that morning with little jars of clotted cream and strawberry jam. A small bottle of white wine and a bar of Charleton House dark chocolate finished everything off nicely. I handed the food and drink over to Molly in a small jute bag with handles and the Fitzwilliam-Scott crest printed on either side, along with a cotton napkin and some cutlery.

'Molly, I meant to ask you: the Duke said that Ambrose had requested a meeting between them, due to take place the day after he died. Did he give you any idea of what it was about?'

She thought for a moment before shaking her head. 'I do

remember that, and I always ask what people want to talk about so the Duke can be prepared, but Ambrose wouldn't say.'

'And this was unusual?'

'Yes. The Duke and Ambrose phoned or emailed each other directly on a regular basis, at least while the exhibition was being set up, so it was unusual for him to ask for a formal meeting.'

Molly thanked me for the bag of food and left me to wonder why Ambrose had changed his usual practice of talking to the Duke in the normal course of work. I could only conclude that Ambrose wanted to be sure they wouldn't be disturbed and the Duke could dedicate a reasonable amount of time to the conversation. He must have had something of importance to discuss and I had no way of finding out what it was.

CHAPTER 26

With a glass of gin and tonic each, Zannah and I were sitting at the kitchen table. We'd eaten dinner, cleared up and were now doing some work. The back door, which led out to a tiny garden with cracked paving slabs and a lot of weeds, was propped open and Penny was sprawled on a stone that still held the heat of the day. A radio play chattered away in the background, but neither of us was paying it any attention.

Once I'd replied to every outstanding email in my inbox (which had numbered an amount large enough for me to need that G&T before commencing work), I watched Zannah's screen.

'Whatcha doin?'

'Putting together a newsletter for the education department volunteers. Their manager is in the middle of recruiting more and is swamped, so I said I'd help.'

'What are those?'

'Photos from the staff garden party a couple of weeks ago. I'm trying to find pictures that have volunteers in them. I know a lot of them, so it's just a question of trawling through the photos to identify them, and then choosing the nicest ones.'

The photos showed a large group of people out on the front lawns of the museum. Many of them had dressed up, but a few still wore their uniforms. Smiling faces beamed at the camera; others had their heads thrown back in laughter, no idea their joy was being caught for posterity. In one, some older ladies had gathered for a group shot, all of them wearing wonderful huge summer hats. They looked as though they belonged at Royal Ascot for Ladies' Day, ready to have a flutter on the horses.

'They do this every year, and every year they get a little more outrageous. They're such a fun bunch. I might put this one on the cover.'

Zannah continued to scroll through the photos.

'Hang on, go back a bit. Stop – that one.' I pointed to a woman in the background of a picture. 'Are there more of her?'

Zannah kept looking and found one. The woman still wasn't the focus of the image, but she was much closer to the camera.

'Her?'

'Yes. Who is she?'

'I've no idea, but she's talking to one of the Botany Department administrators. Tess might know.'

'Can we call her and find out?'

'Oh-kaay.' Zannah sounded curious, but didn't ask me any questions as she put her phone on speaker and called Tess. We listened to it ring.

'Hey, Zan.'

'Hi, Tess, are you free? I'm with Sophie and she has a question.'

'Fire away. Hi, Sophie, how can I help?'

'Zannah is sending a photo over to your phone. I was wondering if you could identify the woman on the left; she's slightly in the background.'

'Sure, okay, I've got it. Let's see...'

There was silence, which went on a little longer than I had expected. Tess either knew the woman or she didn't.

'That's Michelle Orne, Caleb's wife.'

Zannah was still scrolling through the photos on her computer as we talked, and she stopped as she came to one that showed Michelle talking to Ambrose. They were deep in conversation, but looked happy and relaxed.

'Did she come to these events often? Were they not staff only?'

Zannah nodded. 'They normally are, but no one says anything if there are a few people from outside the museum there. She probably just came round to pick Caleb up before going on for dinner or something. Right, Tess?'

Silence.

'Tess?'

'What? Yes.'

'How well did Michelle know Ambrose?' I asked, but again there was silence. 'Tess?'

'Sorry, what?'

'How well did she know Ambrose? Have you any idea?' I reached into my bag and pulled out the photo of the other members of the University Mountaineering Club, holding it up to show Zannah and pointing to a woman standing between Ambrose and Fleur. It was Michelle Orne.

'Tess, are you alright?' Zannah looked concerned and rightly so. Tess had gone silent on us again.

'Yes... no... look, can I come round?'

AN HOUR LATER, Tess's small frame was sinking into an armchair, a large and very strong gin and tonic in her hand. We waited for her to talk, knowing she would say more on her own terms, although I could guess what was coming having seen her argue with Dr Orne. I hadn't told Zannah what I'd witnessed; I'd been distracted by going to Adam's restaurant and had forgotten all about it.

It didn't take Tess long to get to the point. 'I've been seeing

Caleb.' She glanced up at us. 'I know he's married, and I feel awful about that, but it just happened.' There was another pause while she reached out and stroked Penny. 'It was on and off for a while because we both knew we shouldn't be carrying on and he really didn't want to hurt his wife, but when you work together day in, day out, it can be hard to fight that kind of attraction. Michelle used to come to the office if she was in the city and I would find a reason to leave. I felt so bad, I couldn't be around her.'

Not so bad you couldn't call it off, I thought. Having been betrayed in a similar way by Adam and the server, I sympathised with Michelle.

'A couple of times, we talked about the possibility of him leaving her, but it never came to anything.'

'When did this all start?' Zannah asked.

'Last Easter.'

'Wow, so it's been over a year.'

Tess nodded, looking a little tearful. 'I know I've been stupid, but I really liked him, and by the time I found out he'd had affairs in the past, I didn't care. We were having such a good time.'

'And what about last night? I saw you arguing with Dr Orne.'

Tess looked momentarily surprised by this, no doubt unaware that there had been a witness, not least a witness who knew them. Then she sniffed.

'He had just broken it off. Said he couldn't do it anymore. He tried saying it was because he loved his wife, but I'd heard a rumour there was someone else and I asked him about that. He denied it and hit the roof.'

'Do you think there really is someone else?'

She shrugged. 'Maybe, I don't know. It's just a rumour, but there are a few of those going around.'

'So when you found out about his reputation, why did you continue to get more deeply involved?' asked Zannah.

'You know what it's like. When you fancy someone, you ignore all the negative stuff you hear, or you rationalise it. I assumed it was just gossip started by someone whose advances he had turned down, or people who were jealous because he is so good-looking and successful.'

'And what about Ambrose? Did he know about the affair?'

'Yes. He told Caleb to end things.'

'Why would he do that? Caleb's his boss. It's quite a risk to comment on his personal life.'

'They knew each other before they were colleagues, sort of. They weren't friends or anything, but Ambrose went to university with Michelle. I don't know if they kept in touch, but I guess he was looking out for his old friend.'

'What's the situation now? Are you still together, or have you really split up?' Zannah's voice was soft and comforting.

'Oh, it's over. I just wish I didn't have to see him at work. It's going to be awful.' Tess took another tissue from a box Zannah had placed on the coffee table for her.

'Call in sick, take a last-minute holiday. Stay away from the place for a week or so. Caleb won't argue. If anything, he'll be relieved. That way, you can get a break from it all, and go back refreshed and not giving a damn.'

'I thought about that, but I'm worried what he'll think of me.'

'Screw what he thinks!' I declared. 'A married head of department has been having an affair with a member of staff – his assistant. That won't do his reputation any good, and he could get into trouble. Stop thinking about him and look after yourself.'

A COUPLE OF HOURS, more gin and tonic and most of the box of tissues later, we put Tess in a taxi home. After Zannah had closed the front door, she looked at me and shook her head.

'This is one of those occasions when I don't actually like being right. I thought she might be having an affair with him, but they hid it really well.'

'Not well enough to prevent Ambrose spotting it.'

'True. Poor Tess; she was a fool to get involved, but I do feel sorry for her. No one wants to get their heart broken.'

'She's done more than get her heart broken, she's just made herself a suspect.'

Zannah looked horrified. 'Tess? Why?'

'Ambrose wanted Dr Orne to end the relationship, which was the last thing Tess wanted. It was to her benefit to get him out of the way, and she'd have access to his diary. She'd have known that he was going to be at Ravensbury House with Dr Orne. All she had to do was wait around the area until he left, then follow him.'

'The same could be said of Caleb – and please stop calling him Dr Orne, Sophie. I have to think for a moment who you mean every time you mention him. If Caleb was worried Ambrose was going to tell his wife about the affair, then he had a motive, too.'

'And the perfect opportunity. Tess has given us a good reason to suspect them both.'

CHAPTER 27

'Sophie, the Duke has said he'd like to see you when he gets back.'

Molly had come into the café for a coffee as soon as she'd heard me fire up the machine for my third cup of the day.

'Apparently he has something for you and Mark.'

'Any idea what?' She shook her head. 'Okay, I was going to head out, but I'll wait until he's back.'

'His train isn't due in until four, and then he's not going out until seven, so you've plenty of time. And he'll be in a good mood as he's having dinner with Oliver again.'

I placed two foamy mugs of latte on the counter. 'I get the impression that going out with his son is quite a big deal.'

'They haven't had a lot of time together in recent years, they're both so busy. But Oliver's making the most of having his father in London; he's introducing him to a lot of his friends, which the Duke seems to appreciate.'

'Do they not usually get on?' I knew Mark's opinions on Oliver, but I wanted to hear another.

'Oh, you know fathers and sons.' She gave a rather false-sounding laugh. 'They have their ups and downs, but the family is very close.'

As Molly thanked me for the coffee and headed back upstairs to her office, I wondered what Oliver really wanted from his father. I didn't know what was going on between him and Adam, but I doubted it was good. There was every chance that Adam wasn't the reformed man he appeared to be after his time in prison, and if, as Mark said, Oliver was the black sheep of the family, then I didn't feel I was being overdramatic hearing alarm bells ringing in the distance. I'd like to say I wouldn't have the time or the inclination to try to work out what they were up to, but I knew myself better than that.

'Sophie, I placed an order for more coffee, and it should be arriving sometime today. And I've got someone coming to look at the dishwasher; it seems to have a minor leak and I don't want it getting any worse. I've also updated the rota as two of the team wanted to swap days next weekend.'

I looked at Chelsea with what must have been a quizzical expression on my face.

'Was that all okay?' she asked. 'Should I have come to you first?'

'No, are you kidding me? You're brilliant. That's all.'

Chelsea smiled, blushed a little, and then started to arrange a display of scones under a glass dome. She was returning to Derbyshire in the morning and I was going to have to give some serious thought to making sure she had more responsibility back at Charleton House.

My phone rang before I had the chance to get stuck into any other jobs. Joe's name popped up on my screen and I grinned to myself as I took my coffee out to the empty courtyard.

''Ello, 'ello, 'ello,' I said in an overly cheery voice.

'You must be on at least, ooh, your fourth cup of coffee.'

'Third, and you don't sound very happy.'

'I overslept. In fact, I'm still asleep.'

I heard a muffled voice shout in the background.

'Just eat the bloody things,' Joe grumbled in response.

'What's going on?'

'Penance. Like I said, I overslept. If you're late or you stuff up, then your penance is to buy the whole department doughnuts. I went out of my way to get those really good ones from Molly's Bakery, that place that makes its own jam and has the best doughnuts in Derbyshire. Well, it turns out they don't make the mark around here, and now my esteemed colleagues are all complaining that they are wrong. Ungrateful buggers.'

'And you called to tell me that?'

'No, I called to see if you were locked up in the Tower of London as that's the only way to keep you out of police business.'

'Who says I'm not keeping out? The exhibition is doing really well, tickets are selling out each day and the café is busy.' I looked through the glass doors at the quiet café, glad we weren't having a video chat. It was busy most of the time; his call just happened to have coincided with a lull.

'I'm not as green as I am cabbage looking, Sophie Lockwood. I need to know you've not done anything stupid or hacked off whichever detectives are unfortunate enough to have been assigned a murder that happened within a five-mile radius of your place of work.'

'Well, I'm here at the café with a mug of coffee in my hands, so all is well and you can go back to eating doughnuts.'

'I don't believe you, you do know that?'

I paused, not sure which response would combine not lying to my friend with not incriminating myself.

'I'm not in any trouble, Joe, so you don't need to worry.' I wasn't. Not yet, anyway.

'Glad to hear it. Okay, I need to get back to this miserable lot.' I heard another muffled shout in the background.

'Before you go...'

'Yes?' he asked warily.

'I was just wondering about the likelihood of someone being stabbed, but still able to keep walking for a while with no idea it had happened. Have you come across it?'

He gave a loud and dramatic sigh. 'I could just hang up, but, well, I'm too bloody soft. Yes, I have come across that. I remember a stabbing victim who was intoxicated. They didn't realise they'd been stabbed and walked two miles home. I also remember Harnby telling me about someone who got shot in the leg and didn't notice until a police officer asked him why there was blood all over his jeans.' There was a pause. 'Is that it, Sherlock?'

'Apparently, I'm more of a Miss Marple, but yes, that's it. Thank you, Joe.'

'I'm definitely going. Be careful and... oh, forget it.'

I laughed as he hung up. With no handy police officer to confirm the details of Ambrose's murder, Joe's insight was going to have to suffice.

CHAPTER 28

*D*octor Fry had said he could meet me at one o'clock at a café close to Hampton Court station. I dashed around my own café for a couple of hours, then threw caution to the wind and stumped up the cost of a taxi to Waterloo, leaping onto the train with seconds to spare and settling in for the journey. I wished I had more time: the station was a two-minute walk from Hampton Court Palace and I would have given anything to spend the day exploring the magnificent Tudor and baroque building and its beautiful gardens, ending my tour with a drink in a Thames-side pub. But I had to get back to the city in time to see the Duke.

The train trundled through the suburbs of south London as I drifted in and out of sleep, waking long enough to show my ticket to the guard, and then again as we pulled into Hampton Court, the end of the line. Instead of walking over the bridge and up the driveway to the imposing red brick façade of the palace, I turned left out of the station and crossed the road to a rather nice café with a candy-striped awning and seating in its shade.

I recognised Nicholas Fry immediately. He had the healthy glow of someone who spent a lot of time outdoors, a quality that had been captured in the photograph I had of him. He shook my hand, and then called a waitress over to take my order.

'I had been expecting a phone call, but I thought it would be from the police.'

'They haven't spoken to you, then?'

He shook head. 'No, but it is a very long time since I last saw Ambrose. How did you find me?'

I pulled the photograph, which I'd removed from its frame and put in a cardboard-backed envelope, out of my bag and passed it across the table to him. He smiled a little.

'The French Pyrenees. We mainly hiked on that trip, with some climbing thrown in. We had fantastic weather, drank a lot of the local wine, and ate more bread and cheese than I'd ever eaten before. Or since, for that matter.'

'You all got on well, then?'

'When this was taken, yes, very well.'

'I'm guessing that changed. Something must have made you think you'd get a call from the police. What happened?'

There was no deep sigh, no staring off into the distance. He seemed ready to talk about this.

'We had a trip to Italy. We rented a minibus and a couple of us took it in turns to drive. There were six of us: Ambrose, Fleur, myself, a couple of others and a guy called Rob Miller. He wasn't as experienced as the rest of us, but he was keen and he was fluent in Italian. The rest of us could get by – you know, order a pint of beer, point at things we wanted and say thank you, but it was useful to have him around. Some of us were worried about his inexperience, but we all said we'd look out for him, and Fleur was insistent that it would be fine.'

'She knew him well?'

'As far as I know, they were having a fling around this time, but it hadn't been going on for long and wasn't very serious. Well, we'd had a fantastic week, and it was the final day. We finished climbing that afternoon and opened a couple of bottles of wine, relaxed in the sun, took a dip in a river we'd parked up next to. Fleur and Rob said they were going for a walk, that they might do a bit of scrambling.

'An hour later, we decided we wanted to find somewhere for dinner, so we went to look for them. We walked around the corner of a boulder towards a cliff face just in time to hear a crash at the bottom.'

I waited for a moment. 'Rob?'

He nodded. 'They should never have been climbing; they'd already been drinking. I don't know what made them do it and Fleur has never explained.'

'But if he just fell, surely it was an accident?'

'It depends on how you look at it. Safety was the number-one priority of the group. As well as checking our own equipment before a climb, we always checked our partner's. We checked the harness, the knots, making sure everything was safe and secure. Rob had borrowed a harness for the trip and it was quite old. We'd all expressed some concern, but we always checked and double checked it.

'Well, on this occasion, the belay loop had failed. It was clearly bad enough that Fleur should have spotted it and never let him climb. Unless she didn't check because she'd been drinking.'

'Belay loop?'

'It's a loop of webbing on the harness, one of the most important parts as that's where the rope is secured with a carabiner.' I shook my head. 'It's a sort of shackle, a metal loop with a spring-loaded gate.'

'Was she blamed?'

'No, the official report said it was an accident.'

'But the alcohol, it must have shown up in his system?'

'It did, but at the time, the authorities didn't check the rest of us. I'm not sure they would have done anyway, but we all decided we'd say that we didn't know he had been drinking, that the harness hadn't seemed that bad, and that Rob was ultimately responsible for his own equipment and we had taught him what to do. We didn't exactly come out of it looking great – some people said we should have stopped him climbing in the harness at all, but it wasn't as bad as everyone knowing Fleur had been drinking, too.

'Fleur was terrified. We had to calm her down, so we didn't talk about it once we got back to England. It became a silent pact.'

'But why wouldn't you tell anyone what had really happened?'

'Fleur was one of us. We'd climbed in some tough conditions together and we'd forged a bond, so none of us wanted to be the one who told on her. Rob was gone; nothing we did was going to bring him back.'

'But Ambrose felt differently?'

'Not in the beginning. At first, he didn't really say anything, just got stuck into his degree. He stopped climbing, didn't go on any more trips and we hardly saw him. Once I graduated and got my first job at a hospital in London, I never heard from any of the group again. Until a few months ago.'

'Was it Ambrose?'

'Yes, he left a message on my voicemail.'

'What did he want?'

'He wanted to meet up. He said that he had been thinking about the accident and wanted to discuss it.'

'And did you?'

'We didn't meet, but I did call him back. He couldn't talk for long, I'd caught him just before he was due to give a presentation, but he did say that he still felt we'd done the wrong thing by not coming clean, instead putting all the responsibility on Rob. Seems he was haunted by Rob's death, believed we should have taken much better care of an inexperienced climber. I tried to convince him that nothing was to be gained by telling the truth now. Rob's family didn't need the whole thing raked over again. He said he might talk to the others, but I told him not to. They had probably moved on, and he could cause them unnecessary trauma.'

There was no doubt in my mind, but I asked the question anyway.

'Did he talk to the others?'

'I don't know. I didn't talk to him again and I haven't reached out to any of them. I probably should have done after Ambrose died, but they haven't called me, either. It was all a long time ago and I don't feel the need to relive any of it.'

There was no malice in his voice. He didn't seem entirely uncaring, but I would have expected a little more shock or sadness, especially at the way Ambrose had died. There didn't seem to be anything else he could tell me, and I wasn't keen to spend a lot more time with him; there was a bland neutrality to him. I couldn't quite put my finger on it. He wasn't robotic about it all, but the only real emotion he'd shown was when he was talking about the bread, cheese and wine the group had enjoyed in France.

I had one last question for him before I went. 'Why are you prepared to talk to me about this now? It could simply achieve what you've been trying to avoid all these years.'

He didn't give it much thought. 'I'd rather talk to you than the police. They'd hardly join me for coffee overlooking the Thames. And Ambrose is dead, someone has killed him. When I told him nothing had changed, and nor should it, I meant it. But I didn't know he was about to die.'

CHAPTER 29

I sat on the train, waiting for it to pull out of the station, and thought about Ambrose. His search for fairness and justice seemed to have got him into a lot of trouble; in fact, it was increasingly looking as if it had got him killed. Whether the act was in the past or the present – historical research that had been proven fraudulent, the truth behind a tragic accident covered up, or people having affairs and betraying those closest to them – didn't seem to matter to Ambrose. He had been a man of conscience, and someone out there had been determined to make sure their misdemeanours didn't catch up with them.

I was relieved when the train started to move; I would be back at Ravensbury House in plenty of time to meet with the Duke. I also wanted to track down Fleur again. She had some explaining to do.

'SOPHIE, you're here. Marvellous. Is Mark around or is he regaling someone with the contents of his encyclopaedic brain?'

The Duke had walked into the café about an hour after me. Within moments, Mark appeared in the doorway.

'Ah, there you are. Right, let's find somewhere a little quieter.' The Duke led the way up the stairs and into the Fitzwilliam-Scotts' private apartments. Up here, I felt as if everything should be *'Yes, M'Lord'* or *'No, M'Lord',* followed by a curtsy and slow backing out of the room. It was nothing to do with the Duke; he was as relaxed as ever, searching around the sofa and coffee table for his glasses. It was just that sort of environment.

'Got them. Right, you two, pull up a chair over here.'

We followed him to a desk in the corner of the room. It was a beautiful roll top that didn't make a creak or squeak as he revealed the desk area and the myriad of hidden cubbyholes. The Duke took a seat, and Mark and I did as he suggested and pulled over a couple of extra chairs.

The Duke undid the buckle of a leather shoulder bag he had with him. From within, he pulled out an object that was the size and shape of a large, thin book.

'I heard you were interested in this so brought it back for you to look at.' Before him lay a notebook covered in sand-coloured fabric, which had been tucked within a matching pouch. The Duke undid the tie which kept the book closed and opened it up to a random page. The paper was sepia coloured and looked well used. Small cursive handwriting covered the pages.

'Caroline kept many diaries throughout her travels, but this is the one that relates to the period of time covered by much of the work we have in the exhibition. I didn't think you'd want to see the rest. The Natural History Museum did ask if we'd donate the diaries, too, but I want to keep them within our archives at Charleton. I will, of course, allow scholars to access them if need be, but this is one of the few times I'll bring any of them out of the house. I believe you are both returning to Derbyshire later this week so you can take it back with you.'

Mark's eyes were bright and full of curiosity. I knew how much he'd want to get his hands on the diary and spend hours poring over every word. He had introduced me to the joys of historical documents not so long ago, and I was curious too, but Mark would be experiencing a whole different level of interest. I was surprised he hadn't shoved the Duke out of the way and landed on the diary like a slavering, starving dog.

The Duke stood up. 'I'll leave you both to it. I have no idea if the diary will throw any light on the Ambrose situation, but perhaps it will give you a bit more context, and I know you enjoy this sort of thing, Mark.'

I glanced at my friend. I'd lost him to the hands of the historical document gods and I no longer existed to him.

I stood as well and looked at the Duke. 'Let's leave Mark to have some time alone with it. This kind of love should be given a level of privacy.'

He laughed. 'Fair enough. Mark, when you've finished, come and find me. I'll keep the diary in the safe when you're not using it. Mark?'

After a moment's silence, the Duke looked at me and shook his head.

'At least I know he appreciates my efforts. I should go and spend some time with my wife. I'm seeing Ollie again tonight, so I ought to show my face first.'

'Mark, Chelsea will be in the café. Let her know when you come up for air and she'll refuel you.'

Not so much as a grunt. I left him to it. It was time to talk to Fleur.

FLEUR HAD AGREED to meet me at the Southbank, an area of galleries and concert halls that had become a hub for the young and culturally minded. She had been giving an interview at a festival celebrating the achievements of women in the arts and sciences, and was now leaning on a bright yellow railing overlooking the wide pedestrian embankment and the Thames beyond it. The area had become a mecca for skateboarders from around the world. From below came the sound of skateboard wheels trundling along concrete blocks or crashing to the ground as a flip didn't turn out as planned.

Behind Fleur, afternoon drinkers spilled out from the Royal Festival Hall. I'd spent many a pleasant hour there, either listening to talks or concerts inside, or meeting friends for a drink nearby. It felt familiar, like I'd never been away.

Fleur stood up straight as I reached her. 'Sorry for dragging you over here. It's just that I've got a ticket for a talk that starts in half an hour – making the most of a break in my own schedule to hear someone else speak for once.' She gave a nervous laugh that sounded odd coming from such a confident woman. Fleur clearly knew we weren't about to have a social chat, so I decided to cut straight to the chase.

'Shall we walk?' I asked, sure that she wouldn't want anyone overhearing what I had to say. After I'd led the way down some steps and onto the Embankment, we walked past the outdoor bookstalls and the National Theatre. As soon as we'd escaped the crowds and were unlikely to be overheard, I asked her to tell me about Rob Miller.

She nearly stumbled over a child's buggy. 'How do you know about Rob?'

'That really doesn't matter. What does matter is whether or not Ambrose contacted you recently to talk about his death.'

Fleur stood, quiet and still. Eventually, she walked over to the railing and stared into the murky waters of the Thames.

'Rob was a sweet man. A boy, really. We had just started dating, if you could call it that; I don't think either of us was very serious. The whole thing was fun. I'd convinced him to come to Italy with us and he was up for almost anything, although his enthusiasm wasn't matched by experience.

'What happened was an accident. I felt responsible for a very long time; I was meant to look after him, but it wasn't my fault. Not really.' She didn't sound entirely convinced. 'You have to understand, I couldn't have Ambrose telling people about it. He could have ruined the plans for my next trip. I'm completely dependent on sponsorship, and companies wouldn't want to get involved if there was any sniff of scandal. Those that support me would drop me. I couldn't risk that.'

'And Ambrose was threatening to put all that at risk?'

'Yes, yes, he was. He wanted to drag Rob's accident out into the open, talk about it. He said he didn't like that we'd lied, that we'd made Rob look like an alcoholic wild child who didn't care about his own safety. But Rob *was* responsible for his equipment; it was no one else's fault.'

'And the alcohol?'

'That was stupid, I admit it, but we were both adults. I should have known better and so should he. I wasn't responsible for his death.'

'Did Ambrose say you were?'

'No, not in so many words, but I always wondered if some of the group blamed me. They never said it, but that doesn't mean they didn't think it. They forget I was the one holding the rope when he fell. I watched him land. I can still hear the sound of him crashing against the rocks. None of the others saw or heard that, none of them has to live with the memory, and yet I'm sure some still blame me.'

'And do you?'

'It wasn't my fault. It wasn't... I...'

I waited, but she never finished the sentence.

'You must be pretty angry if they're still pointing the finger at you.'

'Yes, I guess. But I didn't take that anger out on Ambrose. Emotions like that I channel into my work, the physical preparation, the planning. When I'm somewhere like K2, I summon every ounce of energy I have to keep going. That's where it all goes, not on killing someone who can't let go of the past.

'I have to go, Sophie. The talk's about to start and I don't want to miss it.'

Without another word, Fleur turned and walked off into the crowds. Now it was my turn to stare into the opaque water of the Thames, wondering who was really to blame for the death of a young man I had never met. I was passing judgements on people I had known less than a week and still didn't know a great deal about. But I was beginning to get a picture of them. The pieces, taken one at a time, didn't look like a lot, but they were gradually falling into place, and together looked a lot more interesting.

A small child on a plastic scooter with a helmet far too big for him ran into my foot, bringing me out of my ruminations. He looked up at me with annoyance in his eyes; I was clearly in his path and, as far as he was concerned, I had no right to be there. I wondered if it had been the same for Fleur. Did she think Ambrose had no right to throw obstacles in her way? She had worked unbelievably hard to achieve all that she had. As much as she denied having anything to do with his death, she'd had a great deal to lose if he'd opened up about the past, and she had the determination and strength to do something about it.

Our meeting hadn't put my mind at rest one little bit.

CHAPTER 30

By the time Fleur had left me on the riverbank and I had considered all the information I had gathered to date, I was getting hungry. Hardly surprising as it was 6pm. I called Mark and Joyce and asked them if they wanted to meet me at the Sherlock Holmes pub; Joyce grumbled, hoping I would choose somewhere a little more classy, but I promised her we would go on somewhere for a cocktail later. With that, she relented.

Fortunately, the pub wasn't too busy when I arrived, most of the customers opting to stand in the open air, otherwise the temperature inside would have been stifling. I was halfway through another uninteresting yet acceptable gin and tonic when Joyce and Mark arrived, looking like the proverbial odd couple. She was sporting bright pink stilettos and matching handbag, her simple cream dress looking either a size too small, or the perfect size for showing off her assets, depending on how you looked at it; he with a moustache that wouldn't have looked out of place in Sherlock's Victorian London, his cream linen waistcoat complementing the image perfectly.

'I don't know why we can't dine on the patio of a fine London restaurant,' stated Joyce, her voice tinged with annoyance. 'You'd better up the ante when we move on.' I had the perfect place in mind that I doubted was going to disappoint her.

Once Mark had joined us with a round of drinks, we ordered our food and we all discussed which versions of Sherlock we had grown up with – in my case, Jeremy Brett, who now formed my only visual image of the great detective as he had been such perfect casting – we moved on to more pressing topics.

Joyce started the conversation off. 'Before Mark talks us through whatever ancient dust-covered news he thinks we're going to find interesting, I have something I need to share with you. I should talk to the police, but I overheard the Duke say that they haven't returned any phone calls he's made and appear to view him as an inconvenience. Anyone who treats our Duke that way isn't top of my list of people to assist.'

Joyce pulled out a spreadsheet covered in numbers that would have made my head spin if it hadn't been for the calming effects of the gin and tonic.

'I've been doing a stocktake of all the letter openers we ordered for London. The shop hadn't opened when Ambrose was killed, so the offending item wasn't purchased by a member of the public. I didn't put them out in the shop until the afternoon of the day he died, which limits further the number of people who had access to them. I gave a couple of them away, but they are all accounted for.'

'Where were they kept until they went on display?' I asked.

'In the room off the kitchen downstairs. We took it over as a storeroom as soon as stock started arriving.'

'So anyone who had access to that room could have taken one. Surely that's a lot of people?' said Mark.

'Quite possibly. It gives us a two-day window between them being delivered to the house and the shop opening.'

Mark was persistent. 'There were a lot of people coming and going during that time, and any one of them could have been sniffing around, found the openers in your stockroom and pocketed one.'

'Or one of the Duke's guests could have got lost on the way to the toilet, found the letter openers and wondered what they were,' I chipped in.

'As could the Duchess's guest – Fleur,' Mark added.

'If you'll just let me finish, both of you.' Joyce eyed us over the glasses she had put on to read the spreadsheet. When she had first been told she would need reading glasses, you would have thought the sky was falling down, but once she realised they were just another opportunity to accessorise, she had cheered up. She was currently peering at her data through bright pink frames that perfectly matched the colour of her handbag and shoes. 'The point of me telling you all of this is that the stock balances perfectly. All the sales match, so we haven't had any go walkabout since the public have been in. I emptied every box in the storeroom and counted them myself, then got one of the girls to count them just to make sure, and everything tallies.'

'What are you telling us?'

'Mark, for a man who looks and sounds like he has swallowed the entire *Encyclopaedia Britannica*, you can be remarkably stupid. What I'm telling you is that the knife didn't come from the stock at Ravensbury House.'

'Forgive my apparently endless stupidity, but where did it come from, then?'

'That is what is causing me some concern. I don't know. There are some extras in my office in Charleton House, and then there were the original samples that I used to sign off the design, but that was months ago. I have no idea where they could have gone since.'

We sat in silence for a moment before I decided to try to sort this new information into something that made sense.

'So, you're saying it has to be a member of Charleton House staff? That one of us who made the journey down here, either to work or set things up before heading back, picked one up from your office in Derbyshire and brought it with them?'

'That's precisely what I'm saying. Whether they did it inadvertently or stole it intentionally is something we have yet to determine. See, Mark, not that difficult.'

Mark rose. 'I'm getting another round of drinks in. It's clearly the only thing I can contribute to this conversation.'

'There's a good chap.' She waved him away with a regal hand.

'Joyce, you are being a little harsh.'

'Far from it. You know it's all said with love, just don't tell him that. And anyway, he'd assume I was unwell if I didn't make the occasional dig.'

She was right. I brought us back to the subject of the murder weapon.

'So what you're saying is that it doesn't mean a member of Charleton staff is the killer. Someone could have brought the knife down for any number of reasons – because they found it useful, or it was just in their bag – and dropped it, which would mean almost anyone could have picked it up. Does anyone from Derbyshire have links with Ambrose? They would have to have known him well enough to have a motive for killing him. The only person I can think of who knew him at all well is the Duke, and I'm not going down that path.'

'So, have you worked out who did it, then?' Mark asked Joyce, sarcasm in his voice. 'You clearly have all the evidence we need on that spreadsheet.'

Wanting to nip the inevitable argument in the bud before it could blossom, I hurriedly filled him in on what we had been discussing. It presented a different avenue to explore, but I wasn't entirely convinced. Ambrose had spent time at Charleton House, but mainly holed up in the archives; he wasn't involved in its life or relationships.

'Is it my turn yet?' Mark was waving his hand in the air like a child at the back of the classroom. I half expected him to be jumping up and down in his seat.

'Oh, calm down, dear. Yes, it's your turn.'

Mark scowled as Joyce patted the back of his hand, then immediately grinned and reached into his rucksack.

'Okay, so, the diary the Duke brought down with him is fabulous. I've really just skimmed the surface, but I've been able to get a good general idea of things with my first reading.' Mark had pulled out a computer tablet that I hadn't seen before. He spotted the curiosity on my face. 'There's a huge store in Covent Garden. I couldn't resist popping out today and treating myself. I can't believe I haven't bought one before. Look, I took photos of all the pages, and now I can read them wherever I am, zoom in and look closely. It's fantastic.'

'You sound like someone's grandfather who has only just discovered tablets exist.' To be honest, he looked a little like one, too, with his pocket watch on a chain. Although he had a smartphone, he was forever putting it down and forgetting it.

Smiling inwardly at the idea of 'Grandpa Mark' regaling us with stories from the past, and almost laughing out loud at the image of Joyce sitting cross-legged at his feet while he did so, I settled down and got ready for him to tell us all about Caroline.

CHAPTER 31

'It's a fascinating read. The woman would go anywhere in search of a butterfly: Guadeloupe, Thailand, Singapore. You name it, she'd pack her things into that tiny suitcase, gather up her paints and brushes, and off she'd go. It was fascinating to see some of her sketches – just quick little pencil drawings, nothing like the paintings we have on display, but they are incredible all the same.'

Mark zoomed in on a couple of photos of the journal. There was a pencil drawing of a caterpillar on a leaf, looking as though it had dozens of arms sticking straight out from its sides, each arm covered in little spikes that resembled needles on a fir tree. A number of sketches of pupae hung from the top of the page or the lines on the paper. The page itself looked stained and a bit grubby; I pictured Caroline sitting under a tree having spent time seeking out those caterpillars and pupae, not minding one bit that her hands and nails were ingrained with dirt.

'Now I checked,' Mark continued, 'and the metamorphosis of some of these species had never previously been captured, or even known about until Caroline made her drawings, so she made a genuine contribution to our understanding of the natural world. She wasn't a big name, but there was recognition of the importance of her work during her lifetime. In 1907, she was invited to join the distinguished Linnean Society and presented a paper to them. That in itself was significant: women had only been allowed to join since 1904.'

I was getting impatient. 'And what of Jacob? You said her letters showed that she had met him in 1889.'

'Yes, they met at a dinner party just before she was due to head to Zanzibar. Caroline dreaded those parties; she hated the fact that travelling with a man might be a sensible idea, but did it all the same.

'Apparently, Jacob was lively company, but after they had been travelling together for a year, she says, *"I am still unclear on what lies at the heart of Jacob's passion. He has great interest in almost everything that crosses his path, but rarely settles on one subject. I am impressed by his capacity to retain almost all and any information; I, on the other hand, must sketch and write in order to record the smallest detail. I must confess to a pang of envy from time to time, not that he will ever be aware of my feelings on the matter."*

'She doesn't say a great deal about his work, but when I searched for him online, I found a lot on his collections. He was really an entomologist, more fascinated by beetles than botany. I do wonder if Gideon plays up Jacob's status in order to make it sound like he's from a great line of botanists, and therefore raise his own status.'

'Was there anything sordid? Anything that might make listening to all this worthwhile?' I'd forgotten Joyce was there.

'Sordid? This is the diary of a Victorian lady explorer, not a Jackie Collins novel.'

'Alright then, is there anything relevant to Ambrose's death? Butterflies are very attractive creatures, but I prefer them made out of diamonds and pinned to a jacket.'

Mark tutted. 'You'd probably stick a pin through the real thing while it was still alive. But to answer your question, no.

Nothing. I'm beginning to wonder if it isn't just plain and simple jealousy on Gideon's part, that's why he's trying to stir things up. He's lucky the Duke is such a laid-back character and isn't confronting him over slanderous comments.

'Listen to what Caroline wrote after Jacob died: *"I will miss his amiable company, his willingness to journey down any street or any rugged path that takes my fancy, and his ability to source some of the finest examples of local cuisine, no matter how remote our location. However, his interest in the natural world extended only to the prettiest objects. With his untimely death, the world has lost a good man with a good heart, but not a great scientist or explorer. He had indeed gathered many items of interest, but his natural tendency was to allow good fortune to find him".*'

'So what does this tell us?' Joyce demanded. 'Other than you've been wasting your time burying your head in books again.'

'It tells us, my darling Ms Brocklehurst, that your admirer is a proud man prone to exaggeration and jealousies, and very possibly flights of fantasy, which I'm guessing he is able to convince himself are true. What it doesn't tell us is that there is a scandalous past which would provide a motive for murder. Yet, Gideon's inclination towards jealousy and fantasy makes me think we should keep him on the list of suspects for the time being. It seems he will do almost anything to protect and rebuild his family's reputation – I can find no suggestion from Caroline that Jacob was a remarkable botanist of any kind, and yet Gideon is convinced that he was, and is prepared to make statements to that effect in front of the Duke and other important people. If he lives in a fantasy land, then who knows what he might think, or indeed do.'

CHAPTER 32

'So, where are you taking me?'

Joyce was pulling her bag up onto her shoulder. She gave her hair a gentle pat, and then stood upright. Her back straight, her chest out, she became a vision that caused a few heads to turn, an effect that she was well aware of and often used to her advantage.

'Just get in the taxi, it's a surprise,' I ordered. Joyce raised an eyebrow suspiciously, but appeared happy to play along.

We were returning to the St James area, a five-minute walk from Ravensbury House. The American Bar at the Stafford Hotel had appeared in the cocktail guidebook Joyce had been reading on the train and she'd expressed an interest. During World War II, it had been popular with serving American officers stationed overseas, and its wine cellars had even been used as air-raid shelters. It continued to wear its history on its sleeve with the memorabilia that adorned the walls and ceiling: baseball caps, club ties and pennants hung above us, the low honey-coloured lighting making them give the impression of an art installation rather than a ragtag display of miscellaneous gifts.

We lined ourselves up at the end of the bar on tall leather barstools.

'Ah, so you've chosen Nancy's place,' the barman said to Joyce with a smile. 'There's only one drink you can have if you sit there.'

Joyce looked as if she was about to dive into the young man's eyes. 'Who would Nancy be and what would she drink?' she asked with a purr to her voice.

'Nancy Wake was a decorated war hero, a member of the French Resistance. The Nazis called her the White Mouse because they could never catch her. She lived here at the hotel for a while, and every evening, she sat at the end of the bar and ordered a gin and tonic. The White Mouse cocktail was made in her honour.'

'Well, Sophie here is your gin and tonic girl. She'll have one of those, I'm sure. To be honest, young man, I'm rather craving a French 75.'

He gave Joyce a polite little nod. 'Of course, madam.' He looked at me and I nodded in agreement with Joyce's order. I was intrigued by the White Mouse. 'And for you, sir?'

Mark was still reading the cocktail menu. 'I'm not sure, what would you recommend?'

'I think a glass of Churchill's Breakfast would suit you nicely, sir.'

Mark folded his cocktail menu and slid it across the bar. 'Then I shall join Mr Churchill for breakfast, I'm sure he'd make a fascinating companion.'

We watched the barman busy himself with our order. Joyce's champagne and gin drink was topped off with a simple twist of lemon; Mark's involved a smoking stick of cinnamon under an inverted glass, which was fun to watch. Mine was made with saffron gin and a star anise floating on top.

Satisfied with her drink, Joyce was scanning the room in case there was anyone of interest. Or, as Mark corrected her, anyone who was rich and single.

'Don't look now,' she whispered none too subtly to us, 'and whatever you do, behave yourselves. The boss is in.'

I attempted to survey the room surreptitiously. At the far end, the Duke, Oliver and a familiar-looking man were enjoying a round of drinks. The man seemed to be holding court, the Duke and Oliver listening intently.

'I thought they were going to the club,' I said.

Mark tried a sip of his drink. 'Mmm, not bad. The Duke has been spending quite a bit of time with Oliver while he's been in London, so maybe he wanted some variety, or they came here after dinner. We're so close to the house, it makes sense.'

The Duke's gathering didn't look entirely social. If I didn't know better, I would have said they were having a meeting, but the Duke had mentioned his pleasure at finally getting to meet so many of his son's friends.

'How is the White Mouse, madam?'

'Lovely, thank you. The saffron is subtle, but delicious.'

Mark took another sip of his drink before speaking. 'I wouldn't mind having this as a local, I'd happily prop up the bar and work my way through the drinks menu.'

His mention of propping up the bar triggered a memory of *Elemental*, the plush restaurant where Adam worked. I'd sat at the bar having a glass of champagne with him. I tried to recall the details of our interaction as it was ringing bells. Looking back at the Duke and his party, I immediately realised why.

The man who was continuing to hold court was the same man who had been hosting the group in the far corner – the group Adam had been rather attentive towards. Was this simply a coincidence? If Adam was involved, then I doubted it.

'Will you excuse me for a moment?' I jumped off my bar stool and went outside.

. . .

THE COBBLED COURTYARD was busier than the inside of the bar. Large modern black planters held an array of foliage, so I tucked myself in a corner out of earshot of any of the other customers or their servers. I still had all the numbers from my days in London in my phone contacts and I scrolled through to Linda's. I didn't want to call *Elemental* directly, so I hoped she'd be on either a day off or a break.

She picked up on the second ring. 'Hey, Soph, I didn't expect to see your name pop up. How's it going?'

'Good, thanks. Look, are you at work? I don't want to get you into trouble.'

'Not a problem, Adam's got me in the office inputting overtime. How can I help?'

'Is Adam with you?'

'No, and if you're checking, then I guess you don't want him to know you're calling?' I heard the sound of a door closing and surmised that she had just ensured some privacy.

'Spot on.' I knew I could trust her. 'That group Adam was looking after when I was at the restaurant on Sunday night – do you remember them?'

'I do, big tippers!'

'Do you know if Adam knew them well? Was there anything about them that stood out as unusual?'

'What sort of thing?'

'I've no idea. I'm wondering if they are caught up in something that affects my employer, but I don't know what or how.'

'Do you mean the Duke and Duchess you work for?'

'Yes.'

'Their son was in here with that group earlier Sunday evening, is that the sort of thing you mean?'

I looked to the sky and muttered a silent thank you. I wasn't losing my mind; there was something about Oliver and his friends that didn't feel right, but I had been worried that I'd spent too long dealing in mysteries and suspicions, and my mind was getting into bad habits.

'Yes, Oliver. He wasn't there by the time I arrived, so what had he been doing?'

'He arrived just after them, had a drink, spent a bit of time talking to one of the men, and then left. He's done that a couple of times. You could probably call him a bit of a regular – gets on well with Adam, enjoys a drink. He only lives round the corner, but we've had to roll him into a taxi a few times.'

'Did Oliver seem to know anyone in the group already?'

'I don't think so. It looked like Adam was introducing him and it all seemed quite formal.'

I wondered what was going on. Oliver seemed to be involved with something to do with Adam, and now I wondered if the Duke was involved, too. Mark hadn't been able to put his finger on exactly what Oliver's line of work was these days, so I couldn't derive any information from that.

'Sophie? Soph, are you still there?'

'Sorry, Linda, yes, I'm just thinking. When was the last time Oliver left drunk, can you remember?'

'A couple of weeks ago, it was Adam's birthday.'

I remembered when that was. I never forgot birthdays, even though Adam was always forgetting mine.

'So 11 June. Did you put him in a taxi?'

'I didn't, and I don't know if anyone else did. He wasn't horribly drunk that time, just tipsy, but he'd had enough that it was noticeable. Adam couldn't get the night off work so he had to restrain himself. Is there anything else I can help you with?'

'No, not at the moment. That was incredibly helpful, thank you. And I'd be really grateful if…'

'…I didn't tell Adam you were asking questions. Don't worry, I won't say a peep.'

'You're a star, thank you.'

'Any time, give me a shout if I can help with anything else.'

We ended the call and I stared at the phone. I wasn't sure if it was the amount of alcohol I'd consumed over the course of the evening, or the information I was trying to sift through, but I didn't feel very clear-headed.

CHAPTER 33

'How's your head?'

Mark looked a little the worse for wear.

'Better than my bank balance. Cocktails are a darned sight cheaper back in Derbyshire.'

'Everything is cheaper back in Derbyshire,' I said, remembering the cost of the taxi I'd decided to splurge out on to take me back to Zannah's. I could feel my credit card wince in my pocket at the memory. 'I hope you've got a light day ahead, you look like you need a darkened room and a cold, damp flannel across your forehead.'

He mumbled a response, the only word I could make out being *coffee*.

'And your plans?' he asked as he rubbed his temples.

'Trying to figure out what's going on with Oliver and Adam, and then how I go about broaching the subject without losing my job.' After another cocktail, and once the Duke and his party had left the bar, I had explained everything to Mark and Joyce. Neither of them had known what to make of it, but both had reminded me to tread carefully.

Mark grabbed a white chocolate and raspberry muffin. 'Right, wish me luck, and check under the stairs before you leave tonight. I might have fallen asleep in a cupboard.'

I WAS grateful that my own head was relatively clear after three large mugs of coffee – or was it four? I'd lost track – when Detective Sergeant Knapp walked in. He was alone and strode towards the counter with a purpose that told me he wasn't here to enjoy one of the rosewater and pistachio meringues that I had just put out on display. They were the size of a baby's head and I had inhaled one within minutes of them being delivered.

'Miss Lockwood, do you have a minute?'

'It's Sophie, and yes, of course.' I took him downstairs to the kitchen and into an empty office to guarantee some privacy.

'DI Grey and I have just returned from interviewing a Dr Nicholas Fry. Does that name ring any bells?'

I felt a cold shiver travel through me and it wasn't because the basement was an icebox even on the hottest days. I feigned deep thought.

'Possibly, I've been catching up with a lot of old friends and acquaintances while I've been back in London. One of them might have introduced me to someone with that name. It sounds vaguely familiar.'

'We've also run into you a number of times at the Natural History Museum. I know you've got friends there and it's open to the public, but it still makes me suspicious.'

I said nothing, I didn't know *what* to say. He sighed and undid his jacket buttons.

'Listen, Sophie, I don't know what you're playing at, but you seem to be paying quite a lot of attention to this case and DI Grey is getting concerned. We both are. You're lucky he's not the one talking to you now. He wouldn't be quite so calm and he might even slap a charge on you for perverting the course of justice. I don't have the time to work out what you're up to, I have a murder to investigate, so consider this a friendly warning.'

I nodded solemnly. 'Can I ask one thing?'

'No.'

'It's just...'

'You can ask, I'm unlikely to answer.'

'Was A... Dr Pitkin stabbed near the house? Did he then walk to the park unaware that he'd been attacked?'

The door swung open and we both turned to look at Joyce.

'Oh, I'm sorry, am I disturbing something?'

'We'd just finished,' said DS Knapp as he walked towards the door.

'Where's the lovely DI Grey? Visiting a manicurist?' DS Knapp looked confused so Joyce wiggled her fingers in the air. 'He really needs to take care of his hands; men shouldn't be afraid of what people might think if they use hand cream or keep their nails nice and tidy. I bet yours are lovely. Let's see.'

'Madam, I don't think...'

'Come on, let me look.' He glanced over at me and I shrugged; resistance was futile. Reluctantly, he raised his hands to where she could see them.

'I knew it. You're a man who takes care of himself. We've already spotted that, haven't we, Sophie?' She ran her eyes up and down his arms. 'And I'm glad to see it extends to your hands. If only your colleague could...'

'Cars,' interrupted DS Knapp.

'Cars?' Joyce looked lost.

'Antique cars. He spends his evenings working on them and can't always get the oil and grease off.'

'Well, he should try harder.'

'I'll be sure to let him know. And, Miss Lockwood, yes.'

'Yes what?' I was confused.

'Yes, he was stabbed here, and in all likelihood was unaware.' With that, DS Knapp made a swift exit.

'Antique cars? Well, he wasn't my type to begin with, but a man who spends all his spare time under the bonnet of a car doesn't appeal at all.'

'That was interesting.'

'Really, Sophie? I didn't think cars were your thing.'

'They're not, but finding out the police went to talk to Dr Fry is. It means they know about the connection with Fleur and they're taking it seriously enough to interview her old university friends.'

Knapp's confirmation of how Ambrose had died was also interesting, and incredibly sad.

The rest of Wednesday morning was steady and the café team worked like a well-oiled machine. Chelsea had done an incredible job of getting everyone up to speed, the young man who had taken over from her proving to be a fast learner who had a great rapport with the rest of the team. Chelsea had already returned to Derbyshire, and I finished on Friday, but when it came to the café, I could relax. Where other matters were concerned, not so much.

I had seen the Duke briefly that morning. He had been so pleased about the amount of time he was spending with Oliver, but I couldn't share that enthusiasm. Oliver was up to something and I worried about Adam's involvement. I didn't like my old world colliding with my new one like this.

'That looks like hard work.'

I looked up at Molly, and then down at the table I was sitting at, confused. She laughed.

'I can practically hear the cogs turning. What's on your mind?'

'Do you have time for a coffee?'

'I do.' She sounded curious, and a little nervous. I got a server's attention and pointed at the empty space in front of Molly. She understood immediately and got to work.

'How well do you know Oliver?'

'Reasonably well. He's a bit of a handful, but harmless. I know he has a reputation for being…well…' She paused, putting a lot of thought into this.

'Come on, Molly, just spit it out. I won't tell anyone what you've said.'

'Okay, well, he's definitely the black sheep of the family when you compare him to the others. He dropped out of university, I've lost track of how many jobs he's had, and he's always appearing online in photos of high-society parties, or the opening of the latest expensive nightclub. I know that some people feel he can be rude to his parents or behave like an entitled brat, but I've always got on quite well with him and I've been able to talk to him when I think he has been out of order. I think he sometimes views me like a sister, one he can boss around and get to run his errands, but he does seem comfortable talking to me.'

'So he doesn't have a set career or interests?' I was trying to get an idea of what sort of thing he could be involved with. 'Has he ever been on the wrong side of the police?'

'Not officially, but there were a couple of occasions when the Duke had a meeting with the family solicitor and wouldn't tell me what it was about, which was unusual. He'll normally give me some idea, even if it's as vague as *discussing the future of the estate.* Those meetings were always followed by a mad hunt for Oliver, who had inevitably disappeared.'

'Recently?'

'No, last year. Things seem to have calmed down since then, but he's probably just behaving himself until he comes up with another madcap scheme.'

'And despite never keeping a job for long, he always seems to have money?'

'Yes. He gets some support from his parents, which I've heard them threaten to pull from time to time, although I don't think they've ever done it.'

'Do you think he'd break the law?'

She laughed. 'I quite like the guy, but I know he'd sell his grandmother if it meant he didn't have to do a regular job.'

The server discreetly placed a mug of coffee in front of Molly, and then backed away. Molly took a sip, and then looked at me, concern etched across her face.

'What do you know that I don't, Sophie? Should I be worried? Should the Duke or Duchess? Has something happened?'

'I don't know. Well, yes, but I don't know what.'

'Can you tell me what you do know?'

I watched her as she took a sip of her coffee. My thoughts returned to what she had said about Oliver and something struck me. I groaned loudly, making a sound reminiscent of a bagpipe being readied. A couple of customers turned, possibly expecting an impromptu rendition of 'Scotland the Brave'.

'I think I know what's happening, and if I'm right, the Duke will be gutted. Quite how I could ever tell him, I don't know.'

'What is it? Maybe I can help you figure it all out.'

'Not here. Let's go into the garden. I don't want anyone hearing this.'

CHAPTER 34

I stood in the garden, looking up at the rear of Ravensbury House and thinking about my employers. No family was perfect, but the Duke and Duchess did a very good impression of a happy couple with a wonderful family. But then, I hadn't seen much of Oliver over the two years I'd worked for them. If my suspicions were right, then they were far from perfect, albeit in a way that a regular family was unlikely to experience.

'Okay, I think I know what is happening. The problem is I have no real evidence, just my suspicions and a few things I have seen. Most parents would defend their children to the hilt without hard evidence, so I could lose my job over this if I pursue it.'

'Tell me what it is, I might be able to help. If I think you're wrong, or that there would be too great a risk to raising it with the Duke, then I'll say so and this will go no further.'

'Okay. Although Joyce and Mark know that I have my concerns, I haven't told them what I think is happening because I only worked it out while we were having coffee.'

'That's interesting. Come on, let's sit.'

We made our way over to a wooden bench. Our backs to the building, we looked out across the manicured garden and beyond to the treetops of Green Park.

'Oliver met and befriended my ex, Adam, at the restaurant Adam runs. It's expensive and trendy, so a lot of the customers will have money and want to make more. I suspect that Adam introduces people to Oliver – people who want to network and make useful contacts who could help their businesses develop. They pay Oliver a large sum of money, a percentage of which goes to Adam as a finder's fee. In return, Oliver introduces these businesspeople to his father over dinner; the Duke is an influential man with a lot of important contacts. Oliver has convinced the Duke that these people are in fact friends of his and the dinners are simply social events. The introduction paves the way for Oliver's "friends" to run into the Duke at a later date and end up having a business conversation. Whatever happens after that, who knows? The Duke is an astute man, so Oliver is taking a big risk, but if – as you said – he'd sell his own grandmother to make money, then he's not beyond using his father for the same reason.'

'You've really seen enough to be certain of this?'

I nodded. 'Sadly, yes. I have a friend who remembers a group I witnessed in the restaurant Adam works at – a group Adam was paying particular attention to – and she saw Adam introducing these people to Oliver earlier that day. I then saw one of them, the one who seemed to be the host of the group, with Oliver and the Duke last night. Mark and I saw Oliver with someone he barely seemed to know outside the Duke's club on Friday; I'd guess he was someone else Adam had introduced him to.

'These aren't friends he's introducing to the Duke; he's met them once, maybe twice before. I've only seen one reference to money in a text, but that is what I think is happening. It's not criminal, he's not breaking any laws, but it's an awful way to use your own parent.'

'It is, and the Duke would be heartbroken. He adores his children. He struggles with Oliver, but still, he's his son and I imagine he'd do anything for him.'

Molly disappeared into her thoughts. I really didn't think there was much more I could do or say. If Molly could think of how to tell the Duke, or at least engineer a way for him to find out 'by accident', then I'd leave that to her. I wasn't prepared to risk my job by tackling the matter directly, and complicated sting operations to manufacture a way for the Duke to stumble across the truth weren't my forte.

'I don't know, Sophie. If you're right, then the Duke needs to know, but off the top of my head, I have no clue how to make that happen. Will you leave it with me?'

I nodded. I didn't feel relieved, either at having worked out what was happening or unburdening myself onto Molly. There wasn't any satisfaction to be found in a single part of this.

'I'm sorry for involving you, Molly.'

'Oh God, don't be sorry. If you're right, then... well, the Duke deserves better than this.'

'My father deserves better than what?'

We both turned to face Annabelle. Neither of us had seen or heard her step out onto the terrace. Just like her mother, Annabelle always looked elegant, her outfit well put together. I'd once seen her walk up the driveway of Charleton House in the pouring rain, her wellies sloshing through puddles and a slick of mud smeared up the side of her trousers and over her bottom where she'd fallen over, and she'd still looked stylish and confident. She could happily have welcomed royalty as she wiped the rain off her face. Now, however, as she stood in a patch of sunlight, her skintight white jeans and loose white shirt made her almost too bright to look at. Her white trainers were spotless.

Annabelle's eyes were hidden behind sunglasses, which she removed as she neared. I could feel the heat that radiated from the stone terrace and wished I could melt away entirely.

Annabelle looked concerned rather than angry, but that didn't do anything to help me relax. For the first time, I felt that my snooping was going to blow up in my face.

Annabelle walked across to the balustrade and leant against it, facing us straight on.

'So, which one of you is going to tell me what is going on?'

AFTER I'D NERVOUSLY REPEATED my suspicions about her brother, I couldn't help but apologise.

'What are you sorry for? You're not my idiot brother abusing our father's trust.'

'So you believe me?' I was surprised.

Annabelle turned and looked out across the garden. After what felt like minutes but was probably only seconds, she faced us again.

'I knew he was up to something, I just didn't know what. He's kept his social life secret for years, but that's not to say I'm completely in the dark. I've seen some of his friends and I often hear what he's up to and with whom, thanks to the jungle drums. The connections spread far and wide in families like ours; everyone is someone's second cousin and it doesn't take much for gossip to travel.

'I've tried to keep an eye on him, mainly for our parents' sake. I don't want him to get into trouble; the press would love that. When he started to spend a lot of time with Father, my trusting parents just thought he had finally grown up. I, on the other hand, remained suspicious. I guess I've always had less patience with him than you have, Molly. I'm much closer to Edward and we've both struggled with our little brother. You're probably a much better sister figure to Oliver than I am. Forever listening to his crazy money-making plans and mopping up after something else fails. I remember he left you to tell that poor girl that their date was off.'

Annabelle clearly saw my eyebrows rise quizzically as she went on to explain. 'He'd got a ticket to the opening of a new nightclub and decided that was more important than keeping a promise to his girlfriend. I seem to recall the poor woman crying on your shoulder, Molly, when you broke the news to her.'

'True, but I felt sorry for the girl. She was clearly besotted with him.' Molly looked across at Annabelle. 'I know, I know, I'm far too soft on him.'

'Yes, you are, Molly. You have a good heart and you let him run roughshod over your generosity and sweet nature. Sophie, would you be good enough to run me through the details again? I want to get this absolutely straight in my mind.'

I had to be careful and make sure I remembered everything. I still felt somewhat intimidated by Annabelle, but it seemed she was on my side. Although that didn't make this situation any more comfortable.

I took a deep breath and retold everything I had seen.

CHAPTER 35

'Bloody hell, you were lucky.'

Mark's hangover seemed to have cleared and he was thoroughly perky as he bounced up the front steps into the Natural History Museum. He had insisted we visit the botany library and I wasn't going to argue if there was a chance it could be useful.

'She could have turned round and told you not to spread such salacious rumours about her brother and fired you on the spot.'

'Annabelle isn't technically my boss.'

'No, but she could have told her father to fire you, and he probably would have done if neither of them believed you.'

'Are you saying you don't believe me?'

'No, far from it. It all adds up to me, and if Molly and Annabelle are also onside, then I think you're on pretty solid ground. I just don't want to be anywhere near Ravensbury House when she tells the Duke what has been going on.'

'Well, let's hope she does it while we're here at the museum and well out of reach. Or even better, after we've left London and are hundreds of miles away in Derbyshire.'

A group of overexcited schoolchildren shoved past us, emitting high-pitched giggles and screeches as they spotted the skeleton of the whale. A couple of them bumped into Mark. He growled at them and they stepped away quickly.

'Leave the poor things alone.' I texted Zannah to tell her we had arrived, and then watched as the children's teacher attempted to get them into some kind of order.

'How's Tess?' I asked as Zannah led us through a warren of beige corridors that reminded me of a hospital.

'She ignored our advice to take time off, but she's fine, currently wondering if she'd be better off with a woman and trying to convince me to go to a lesbian bar with her.'

'And will you?'

'Sure, but it will never happen. She'll either decide that Caleb isn't so bad after all, or she'll lay eyes on some other handsome botanist and spend her time trying to find out if he's single. Okay, here we are. Usual rules: no food, no drink. Michael, one of the librarians, is usually at his desk in the far corner and can help with anything you need. Send me a message when you're done. I almost forgot, here are your passes. Have them on display all the time. Ta-ra.'

She gave a little wave as she walked away.

'Right,' declared Mark. 'Let's find this Michael chap and crack on. I think I'm onto something, but I want to be certain.'

In no time at all, we were surrounded by piles of books and reports, spread out across a long wooden table in the middle of the room. Mark spent the next couple of hours poring over them, occasionally handing me books with instructions on what to look for. We could find nothing that marked Jacob out as a botanical explorer, or anyone of particular note. But that didn't matter to Mark. He had his sights on something else.

'I was reading about Jacob Snable-Bowers online this morning. I accessed a couple of different archives and the records often referred to his home in Scotland, or at least one of the family homes being in Scotland. Gideon's family were loaded back then, they had property and land all over the place. They were clearly useless with money to lose all that. I hope Joyce isn't really interested in him, he'll probably spend all her money and they'll be living out of the back of her car in no time.

'Anyway, all this started to ring some bells, and then I remembered the case of fraud that Tess told you about, from the 1930s.' He spread out a number of spiral-bound pages. 'These are various reports that have been written over the years about Roger Ferguson's research.'

The mass of books and papers and the old style library made me feel as if history was likely to start seeping in through my pores. Bookshelves covered every inch of wall space, ladders on railings waiting patiently for someone to climb them and explore the treasures that were out of immediate reach. Above us, a balcony that gave access to even more shelves ran along all four walls, a beautiful iron spiral staircase tucked away in one corner leading up to it. More ladders were up there, ready to be pulled around. I imagined propelling a ladder at speed and clinging on as I shot along the wall.

Mark stuck a pencil in my arm. 'Are you listening?'

'Sorry, yes. This place is amazing.'

He grinned, happy that he'd passed on a love of dusty books and hidden histories to me last Christmas when we had researched a historical murder.

'Come on, then, pay attention. The more I read about Gideon's ancestor, the louder the bells rang. I'm sure there is a connection between the two cases.' A fire had been lit in his eyes and it glowed as he grinned at me again. 'I've only had time to scan some of these pages, but I can see that I'm right.

'Tess told you, as I recall, that a well-respected botanist in the 1930s was found to have transplanted rare grasses from his own garden to an area in Scotland. That botanist, Roger Ferguson, had special access to the land with the agreement of the landowner – a very wealthy aristocrat with houses and land all over the place. That landowner was Ichabod Snable-Bowers, grandfather of our very own Gideon.'

He looked up at me gleefully. 'Incredible, right? This was right under our noses.'

'I just love the name Ichabod. I think that's what I'll name my next cat. Ichabod.'

'Can you please stay on track?'

'Sorry. And you're sure Ichabod knew what Ferguson was up to?'

'No, I'm not sure, but I might be able to find out more in amongst all this.'

'But Gideon's father lost a lot of the family property years ago, and more went as they struggled under his gambling debts, so Gideon isn't linked to any of this. Besides which, he's far too young to have been involved in a fraud from the 1930s.'

'Agreed, but he's desperately trying to rebuild the family portfolio and increase the standing of the Snable-Bowers name once again. Joyce said that he's clinging on to all possibilities, including the idea that an ancestor actually wrote the work attributed to William Shakespeare. The man is clearly desperate. He couldn't find any evidence to show that Jacob was a noteworthy explorer, but even more damaging would be evidence that his grandfather was involved in fraud.'

'So...' I was running through it all in my mind. 'Gideon is trying to reinstate his family name, and along comes Ambrose, who starts digging around this historic case involving Gideon's family history. What Ambrose is keen to bring into the spotlight is a case of scientific fraud which he might be able to prove that Gideon's grandfather was fully aware of. That's hardly going to enhance the family's good name. Ambrose was a man forever in pursuit of justice and truth, so would not be prepared to drop it. Gideon tries to convince him to let it go; perhaps they have another conversation about it as they leave Ravensbury House after dinner, where Gideon has been reminded of the world he so desperately wants to be a full and active part of. Ambrose won't back down, Gideon has had a few drinks, and in the heat of the moment he stabs Ambrose with a letter opener that he just happens to have picked up during the evening. Although we still don't know exactly where the killer got the letter opener from as Joyce has been able to confirm that none are missing.'

'That's what I'm thinking, but I really need to find evidence that Ichabod knew what was going on.'

'Does this mean the whole Caroline and Jacob story no longer matters?'

Mark nodded. 'I don't think that Gideon's obsession with a story that has been passed down through the generations matters at all. Because that's all it is: a family myth. But I do think we should talk to him about Scotland. It's time to bring in the big guns.'

'The what?'

'Our secret weapon, which no man can resist. And if they do, they'll face a wrath like no other and a rather terrifying set of nails that can slice through their jugular quicker than they can say, *"Get the mad woman off me".*'

'Joyce?'

'Of course I mean Joyce. She's been cosying up to Earl Penniless, so it's time we got her to use her charms for the benefit of others.'

'What are you thinking?'

'Didn't you say that she's got another date?'

'Tonight, yes.'

'Then we'll gatecrash. We'll tell her, of course; I don't want to find myself clutching my neck and bleeding to death because we've interrupted whatever the dragon lady's version of an intimate moment is. Cornered, Gideon will likely reveal all.'

'And if he doesn't?'

'We leave him to die a slow and messy death at the hands of his date.'

ONCE MARK HAD MADE some more notes, and I'd been told off for climbing one of the ladders that had proven far too tempting, Zannah escorted us out of the library. We wound our way back through a myriad of corridors and out into a sudden cacophony of screaming schoolchildren which took Mark and me by surprise. I'd forgotten about that less desirable side of museum life. Our ears ringing, we concluded that it was close enough to 5pm for us to permit ourselves to hold our debrief in a nearby pub, and set off up the congested Cromwell Road. It wasn't hard to understand why this road had some of the most polluted air in the country.

As we turned a corner, I spied something up ahead that caused me to stop mid stride. Mark spun round.

'Are you alright?'

'Fine, but encountering him is becoming a little too common an occurrence.' I nodded towards the side road that ran next to the pub we were heading for. It led to an underground station, and just outside stood Dr Caleb Orne.

I held Mark back. 'If past experience is anything to go by, he generally isn't a positive omen. Let's watch, just for a minute. He must be waiting for someone to get off the Tube.'

'You know there's a pint with my name on it, waiting patiently for me on the bar, a beautifully cold drop of condensation sliding down its side, glistening in the summer sun.'

'If it's on the bar, how can it be glistening in the sun? I'll buy you a bag of crisps if you shut up.' He mimed zipping his mouth shut. 'There... dammit! I can't see them.'

Caleb had turned as he'd spotted someone. He was talking to them, but they hadn't stepped far enough out of the station entrance for me to see their face. It looked as though he had gone in for a hug, but had been rebuffed as he stepped back.

'Come on, come out a bit further. Only a foot,' I implored the hidden person.

'We could go down the street, move this thing on...'

'There's nowhere to hide, so we'd be spotted.'

'Who says the other person would recognise us?'

'It's not a risk I'm prepared to take. We're already far too exposed here, they only have to look this way and... oh, hell!'

'What? Who is it... oh! Oh, wow!'

I allowed myself to fall back against the grubby grey wall of a bank and looked heavenwards.

'Uh-oh, Soph, she's spotted us.'

I looked down the road and locked eyes with Molly Flinders.

CHAPTER 36

'And this means what, precisely?'

Mark's first pint had an inch left in the bottom which he was nursing. The nearest pub into which we'd dived after scurrying away from our shock at seeing Molly meeting up with Caleb, happened to be The White Lion, which Caleb had informed me was one of Ambrose's regular haunts.

'I guess it doesn't have to mean anything. She could just be another one of Caleb's women. She's had plenty of opportunities to meet him at Ravensbury House, and I know she's taken paperwork related to the donation of Caroline's paintings to the museum on behalf of the Duke. And she lives here. She's attractive, he's got a track record.'

'So, why exactly did we run away like a couple of naughty schoolkids?'

'Not sure, really. I just don't like the idea of her meeting with someone who could conceivably be a killer. And what if Caleb saw us, too? He started to get suspicious when I quizzed him at the herbarium; I don't need him realising we might be onto something…'

'And coming after you with a letter opener,' Mark interrupted with a grin.

'Take this seriously, Mark, it's murder we're talking about.' Mark mimed zipping his lips, the humour still gleaming in his face, and I rolled my eyes at him. 'And anyway, we don't know yet if he's even the killer.'

Mark nodded. 'I must say, I like Molly. I was talking to her the other day about how she should come up to Charleton more often. I'd give her a guided tour, then we could go for lunch at the Black Swan. But I'm not so keen now.'

'Remember, she's not the one having an affair, assuming that is what's going on. She's single, so she can date whoever she wants. He's the one being unfaithful, so that side of things is his problem.'

'Do you really think that? Would you get involved with a married man?' Mark asked.

I thought for a moment. 'No, I wouldn't. But I guess you can't control who you fall in love with, so who knows what any of us would do in the heat of the moment under certain circumstances? I'd like to think I wouldn't, but I suppose I can't say 100%.'

Mark downed the rest of his beer and stood up. 'I need another one. You?' I nodded.

While he went to the bar, I thought more about Molly. I really was in no position to judge, and the next time I saw her, I would treat her just as I always had.

'Do you think we should still let Joyce go out with Gideon tonight?' I asked as Mark placed two glasses on the table.

'You want to be the one to try and stop her?'

'No, I thought maybe I'd send you to do the deed.'

'And I thought you liked me! Why not? Do you think we're knowingly letting her go on a date with a killer?' He didn't look too concerned.

'Maybe. Whether the spur was Jacob laying claim to Caroline's discoveries, or Roger Ferguson's fraud, the possible motive remains the same: protecting the family name, which we know Gideon is passionate about.'

'True, but everything you've told me about Fleur points the finger of suspicion pretty firmly in her direction. Plenty of people could view her as responsible for that lad's death. That's a lot worse than replanting some grass, which is old history. If it got out that Fleur was drunk while she was on the other end of that rope… She's a feisty, determined woman who climbs mountains so high, I get altitude sickness just looking at pictures of them. I really would not want to run into her on a dark night; she doesn't look like much, but she's what our American cousins would call the proverbial tough cookie.'

He was right.

'Come on.' Mark sounded encouraging. 'Let's get it over with, tell the lovely Joyce that she can't rely on becoming a countess any time soon.'

He pulled out his phone and called Joyce, putting her on speakerphone.

'I thought I'd blocked your number, it seems I'll never be rid of you.'

Mark slid the phone towards me.

'You talk to her, I have no interest in saving her from a life as a prison widow.'

'Sophie, are you there?'

'I'm here, Joyce. Sorry to disturb you, but we need to talk to you.'

I glanced around the tiny beer garden with its tall concrete walls, brightened by dozens of hanging baskets, the sound of traffic a low hum. One old bloke was absorbed in a newspaper in the far corner. There was no one to pay any attention to our conversation.

'Well, I've just finished for the day and am on my way to the apartment to get ready, so you can talk as I try and get a cab.'

'It's about tonight.'

'Don't tell me, I'm about to go on a date with a murderer?'

Mark and I looked at each other.

'Well, that pause just told me everything I need to know.'

'No, no, we can't prove anything yet, but we have pretty strong suspicions.'

'What Sophie the super sleuth is trying to tell you is that your Earl is currently on our list and we need to gatecrash your evening.'

There was silence from the phone, and then, 'He is a bit boring, and I have a suspicion he's expecting me to pay for dinner tonight, so tell me what you want to do. I'm in.'

MARK GATHERED our empty glasses and we walked into the pub. There was no exit from the yard at the back.

'I've just had a thought,' I told Mark as I indicated to the barman that we'd returned our glasses.

'Go easy there, you don't want to strain something.'

I ignored him and continued to wave the young barman over. Taking advantage of a lull in custom, he walked to our end of the bar, dressed in a white t-shirt and jeans full of holes. Pulling up a photograph of Ambrose from a newspaper article on my phone, I showed it to him.

'This is a friend of ours, he used to come in here quite a lot. I was wondering if you remembered him.'

'Yeah, of course. He worked at the museum – wasn't he killed last week?'

'He was. Do you remember seeing him recently?'

The barman reached for our glasses while he thought. 'Not for a while, but he was like that. Some weeks he'd be here every day, then we wouldn't see him for ages. Off on trips abroad, I think he said, something to do with his job or conferences, that sort of thing. He was nice enough.'

'The last few times you saw him, did you notice anything about him? Did he seem worried or distracted?'

The barman smirked. 'The last time he was 'ere, I noticed something alright, but he wasn't worried, he was mad as hell. He came dashing in and demanded a *strong drink* and to *make it a double*. Kept cursin' someone, calling him a *bloody fool*. Said he'd nearly been knocked flying by someone who'd shot through a red light as he was crossing the road outside, adding, *"Just wait until I see him"*, so I guess it was someone he knew. He wasn't hurt, though, and calmed down eventually. I didn't see him again.'

'What time was this, can you remember?'

'Fairly late, about nine. It was a Friday night, so it must have been...' he looked over his shoulder at a wall calendar showing the whole year, 'the eleventh, I guess, 11 June. He said he'd been at a work event.'

'Did he say anything about the driver? Anything that might identify him?'

He shook his head and started pulling a pint for a customer who had just sat at the bar.

'Not that I can remember.'

'Okay, thanks. Caleb?' I suggested to Mark as we left the pub. 'Saw him crossing the road and decided to warn him off interfering in his private life by scaring him?'

'Perhaps. He referred to the driver as him, so we know it was a bloke. It could have been Gideon.'

'Hang on.' I quickly dialled Joyce's number.

'What now?'

'Sorry to disturb you again, Joyce. I was wondering, does Gideon commute around the city by car?'

Joyce snorted. 'Car? You've got to be kidding. Turns out the sap doesn't even know how to drive.'

'Thanks, Joyce, I'll leave you alone now.'

I hung up. If we'd been back in Derbyshire, I could have asked Joe to check the traffic cameras in the area to see if the incident had been captured, but since DS Knapp had warned me off, I couldn't talk to him about it. This was something I was going to have to figure out by myself; I instinctively knew it was important. It was far too much of a coincidence for me to ignore. It also, I noted, ruled out Fleur.

CHAPTER 37

I watched as Mark jumped into a taxi, having told him that I was going home to change. But I had something I wanted to do first.

I found Molly in her tiny office on the first floor of the house, between the Duke and Duchess's kitchen and sitting room. I knew our employers were out and wouldn't be back until after dinner, but I still crept along the corridor nervously as though I was doing something untoward.

The office door was open. Molly's back was towards me as she pored over some documents on her desk. Her head rested in a hand and her whole posture looked tired and defeated. Next to her keyboard was the paperwork relating to the £100 speeding fine she had to pay.

I tapped lightly on the doorframe and she sat up with a jolt.

'Oh God, Sophie, don't do that!'

'I'm sorry.'

'It's okay.' She took a moment. 'I wondered if you'd come and find me. Let's go somewhere we can both sit; this place is so small, I can't shut the door without contorting my body in ways it wasn't designed for.'

As we walked through to the sitting room, I took a good look at her. Her shoulders seemed to be slouched in a way I hadn't spotted before and she had lost the healthy glow that reminded me I needed to spend more time outdoors.

'Are we okay in here?' I asked, still feeling guilty and out of place. Molly nodded.

'They won't be back for hours and no one will disturb us.'

We sat at opposite ends of the long cream sofa, Molly picking up a cushion and holding it against her stomach.

'I guess I should explain.'

'You don't have to, it's none of my business.'

'Maybe, but I've felt dreadful about it for months. I know there's no excuse, but it's not quite how it looks and I don't want you to come to some dreadful conclusions about me.'

She fiddled with the trim on the cushion, avoiding any eye contact.

'I met Caleb last year when I accompanied the Duke to a couple of meetings with him and a few others from the museum. Then there was a drinks reception at Christmas where we got chatting, and after that we started to email. It went from there. I didn't know he was married in the beginning, I swear. I'd never have got involved if I'd known. When I did find out, I didn't see him for weeks, but at Easter things really began to come together for the donation of the paintings to the museum, and I had to have contact with him again. I could hardly tell the Duke why I didn't want anything to do with Caleb, could I?'

She looked at me and I shook my head to reassure her. She was right. This wasn't something I would have shared with him either.

'Caleb suggested we go for a drink. I stupidly accepted, and it all started up again.' She closed her eyes briefly.

'What did he say about his wife?'

'He didn't say he was going to leave her, if that's what you mean, but he was really conflicted. For a while we were off and on, and it was horribly stressful. I think I was waiting for the exhibition to be over, the paintings to be donated, and then there was no reason for our paths to cross again. That's what today was about. We were meant to go for an early dinner, but I told him I didn't want to see him again.'

Molly looked genuinely exhausted by the whole thing. It was jarring to see this well put together, super-organised woman suddenly look so tired. I wondered if she knew about Tess and the other women Caleb was rumoured to have had affairs with, but it didn't really matter. I figured that if she didn't already know, then she didn't need to; it would hardly make her feel any better.

'What are you going to do?' I asked. It took her a while to answer, but she was able to give me a weak smile as she spoke.

'Try and keep my head down until the exhibition is over. I will still have to deal with him, but I'll make sure we're never alone together. Anything to ensure I don't give in to temptation.'

'Well, let me know if I can do anything to help. I often go to the museum to see my friend, so I can deliver paperwork for you.'

'Thanks, Sophie, I appreciate it. And thanks for not judging me.'

I shrugged. 'I'm far from perfect.' I leant across and gave her arm a squeeze. 'Why don't you go home, have a hot bath, or a glass of wine? Something to help you relax.'

She nodded. 'That sounds like a good idea, I will.'

I stood up, prodding the cushions I'd been leaning against back into shape, feeling like I should hide all evidence that I had been in this part of the house. After giving Molly a quick hug, I went to collect my things. I needed to go home and change; I had a hot date to get ready for, just not my own.

CHAPTER 38

'Blimey, he does get around! His poor wife, I wonder if she has any idea at all.'

Mark and I were in a coffee shop around the corner from the Savoy. Joyce had insisted that she and Gideon return there for a cocktail after dinner, although she had promised to pay, and we were killing time until she sent us a message to confirm they had arrived.

'I hope she finds out and rips his... well, you know what I mean.'

'I do and I agree. I'm surprised at Molly, though; she always seemed more sensible than that.' He was right, but I guess that just made her human. 'Hang on, if Tess being involved with Caleb made her a suspect, doesn't this make Molly one, too?'

'Yeah, I hadn't thought of that.' I tried to imagine Molly caught up in anything other than an inappropriate relationship and struggled. 'She's incredibly loyal to the Duke and Duchess. She wouldn't risk that.'

Mark shook his head. 'No, I don't think she would, either. I just hope she can make a proper break from Caleb and avoid getting mixed up with him again. You'd think she'd have her pick of wealthy eligible young men at all the events she arranges for the Duke and Duchess. Speaking of which... well, maybe not young. Or wealthy, come to think of it...' He glanced at my phone, which had lit up with a message from Joyce. 'Come on, the spider has her fly trapped in the web. We'll head up Farting Lane.'

'I beg your pardon?'

'Farting Lane, it's over here.'

I followed him to the bottom of a steep, narrow lane which was clearly marked *Carting Lane*. I pointed at the sign.

'You child.'

He grinned. 'Yes, I'm happy to confess to possessing a rather childish mind when it comes to humour, but on this occasion, it's more than that. Ta-dah!' He swept his arms wide and presented to me a Victorian street lamp. 'This is London's only remaining sewer lamp. They were used to burn off the smells and germs from the sewers, and in a masterstroke of multi-tasking, they could be used as gas lamps at the same time. This one was powered using the methane gas from the waste of the guests at the Savoy.' He pointed at the building next to us. 'It was quite literally fart powered.'

'And now?'

'Electric like all the others. Cool, eh?'

'Something like that.' I screwed up my face. 'Come on, the spider will be getting restless.'

We walked down the tiny street that led to the hotel doors, famous as the only street in the country where vehicles were driven on the right hand side, and into the Art Deco lobby. I was very pleased I'd made an effort and worn my go-to summer party outfit of loose cream trousers and a sleeveless silk top that had swathes of pastel colours across it, and I'd changed my workaday black-framed glasses for a pair with a pale blue frame. Mark had once told me that in this top, I looked like I'd been attacked by a gang of angry paintbrushes. He looked as if he'd been born to belong here in a linen trouser and waistcoat outfit, a spotted bow tie finishing off the look perfectly.

I linked my arm through his and he led the way to the Beaufort Bar. I immediately spotted Joyce and Gideon at the bar; she was perched on a tall stool with her legs crossed seductively, her skirt so short I had to double check she was wearing one. There was no doubt about it, she had legs that deserved to be shown off to the world. The black paintwork, the golden glow of lighting, the gilding behind the booths that lined one of the walls – it was theatrical elegance in the extreme. The sounds, smells and sights of one of the world's busiest cities instantly vanished.

'Sophie, Mark, how wonderful to see you here!' Joyce slid off her stool in a surprisingly graceful move. It turned out that she wasn't wearing a short skirt at all; instead, a long black chiffon number with a side split all the way to the top of her thigh had blended in with the black paintwork of the bar. Now it swirled around her ankles, setting off her gold high-heeled sandals. A thick gold belt separated the skirt from a simple black vest, and her cleavage was partly hidden by so much gold jewellery, I wondered why she didn't have her own personal security guard. Of course, I knew that none of it was real, but the effect was that she didn't just look like a well-dressed customer, she looked as though she owned the place. 'I heard you say you wanted to come here for a drink, but how marvellous that we're all here together. Gideon, you remember Sophie and Mark?' Gideon shook Mark's hand and kissed me on each cheek. I couldn't tell if he was surprised or perturbed. 'Why don't we move to a table? Gideon, would you bring my drink over?'

We settled ourselves around a low black table and a server came and took a drinks order for Mark and me. I kept an eye on Gideon. Although he was exchanging pleasantries with Mark, he didn't look entirely comfortable. I wondered if he had realised that this was a set-up.

'I was in the Natural History Museum's botany library today,'

Mark declared as our drinks were placed on the table. 'Fascinating place, and such a remarkable collection. I could spend weeks in there.'

'I've spent a little time in there myself,' Gideon commented. 'But I'd much rather get my hands dirty.'

'I'm afraid that's not quite my style.' Mark laughed, Joyce and I joined in. I couldn't begin to imagine Mark on his knees, working on a flowerbed. 'But then, the passion for botany rather runs through your veins, doesn't it, My Lord?'

'Call me Gideon, please, and yes, you could call it the family business.'

'Yes, your family name came up a few times. I was impressed to see that one of your ancestors had crossed paths with the likes of Carl Linnaeus and Peter Collinson.'

Gideon shuffled in his seat, but smiled proudly. 'Yes, my family always enjoyed cultivating our gardens and often sought out the newest specimens as they arrived in England.'

I relaxed a little; I would allow Mark to run the conversation for a while. As they spoke, I looked over at Joyce. She caught my eye and gave a slight nod.

After a lot of talk about botanical adventurers from the 18th century, I decided to bring things to our intended conclusion and chipped into the conversation.

'I was reading about a fascinating case, up on the northwest coast of Scotland. Near Skye, I think. I had no idea there was such a thing as fraud within the botanical world, but I suppose I shouldn't be surprised to find it everywhere in life.'

Gideon's eyes flicked my way at the mention of Skye.

'Quite. Although I don't think that case was of particular interest to most people. It sank without a trace, so I don't think there was a great deal of evidence.'

'Really? The article I read said there was quite a lot of evidence. I was surprised that a bigger deal wasn't made of it.'

Joyce screwed her face up in a farcical display of concentration, before reaching over and putting a hand on Gideon's thigh.

'Gideon dear, didn't you mention Skye the other day? I'm sure you did. You said you'd visited or had some connection with it.'

'I don't recall,' he muttered. 'Perhaps. We have connections all over the country, so it may have come up.'

I sat quietly waiting. Mark was getting into the swing of things.

'I believe the area was quite important in relation to some rare grasses, although as a botanist, I'm sure you're well aware of all that. It's probably old news?' He looked genuinely curious and I briefly wondered if theatre had played a part somewhere in his family history. I knew it had in Joyce's, but Mark was the one putting on an impressive show at the moment.

'What's going on?' Gideon put his glass on the table firmly. 'I sense you are making some sort of a point. Yes, my family had an estate on the mainland, just across from Skye. Joyce, are you involved in this?' There was a mixture of frustration and disappointment in his expression as he looked at his date. Joyce managed to keep a look of sweet innocence on her face.

Mark replied calmly, 'Not at all, I was just curious. It's a fascinating story, although I am a little surprised that it was buried. It's the sort of thing that I imagined would have gained much greater attention.'

Gideon shot up out of his seat. 'I've clearly been set up. I'm not wasting another moment of my time.'

'Gideon dear, sit down. There's no need to overreact, you're amongst friends.' Joyce took his hand and pulled him back into his seat. He landed like a sack of potatoes.

'Oh, for heaven's sake. Yes, it was my family's estate that Roger Ferguson transplanted the grasses to, but we weren't involved.'

'Are you sure about that?' Mark leant forward, looking like a

TV detective who had a suspect on the brink of confessing. He was getting a little too into character.

'What would we have to gain by hiding a thing like that? It was ninety years ago.'

'Yes,' I added, 'but let's not forget how keen you are to reinstate your family name. You plan to get back as many of the properties that your father lost as possible.'

Gideon glanced at Joyce. He now knew that she'd been spilling the beans. He signalled a server over and ordered a glass of scotch. We sat in uncomfortable silence until the drink arrived, Gideon snatching it from the server's tray before he'd had the opportunity to place it on the table. After he'd knocked back the entire glass in one go, I looked him in the eye.

'Did Ambrose talk to you about this?' I asked. Gideon sighed.

'Yes, yes, he did. I have no idea why, but he'd got a bee in his bonnet about it. Felt that Ferguson's actions had been wrongly swept under the carpet. He even talked about carrying out more tests that proved Professor Judd's theories. You see, the grasses in Ferguson's garden were never actually examined in order for the case to be 100% proven. The London School of Botanical Studies decided to bury the whole story before that could be done; they didn't see the point, and they certainly didn't want to throw our field of study into disrepute.'

'And that also helped to avoid dragging your family's name through the mud,' I chipped in.

'My grandfather had no idea what had happened. He allowed Ferguson onto the land in order to study the plants there; he had no idea what the man claimed to have found until he was contacted by someone investigating the fraud who wanted to interview him about Ferguson's work.'

'That's not quite true, though, is it?' Mark looked annoyed. 'Once I knew what I was looking for, it wasn't hard to find reports of Ichabod being actively interested. He even gave an interview to the local press about what a privilege it was to have

Ferguson working on site and how fascinating it was to learn more about the land that had been in the family for centuries.'

'That doesn't mean that he knew what Ferguson was up to,' Gideon growled.

'No, but it's enough to arouse suspicions, and it would be really unfortunate if Ambrose brought all this out into the open just as you're trying to make your mark on society again, put the name Snable-Bowers up there with the Fitzwilliam-Scotts of the world.'

Gideon leant forward and, with a low snarl in his voice, jabbed a finger in Mark's direction. 'How dare you! I know what you're insinuating, and how dare you! I left Ambrose with the Duke and went home that night; I did not kill Ambrose. How dare you suggest such a thing, and how dare *you!*' He turned to Joyce, who flung her hand to her chest in a dramatic display of innocence. 'I genuinely liked you, Joyce, and I'm extremely hurt that you could collude with these... these...'

Unable to find a suitable insult, he stormed out of the bar.

CHAPTER 39

Joyce sat opposite me in the café and took a sip of her drink before handing me two fifty-pound notes.

'What are they for?'

'You wouldn't accept my money last night, so I'm hoping that in the clear light of day, you'll realise how silly that was and will take it now. Either that or your bank manager will phone you and enquire as to whether you've just bought yourself a brand new car, which is what I'm assuming the bar bill could have cost you.'

She wasn't far wrong.

'It's fine, honestly, put them away.'

'If you won't accept them willingly, I am going to staple these notes to the back of your hand.' Her eyes drilled into mine. I knew my place.

'Okay, thank you very much, it's very kind of you.'

'Pah! I don't want to see you eating baked beans for the next couple of months. So, do you think he did it?'

'I should be asking you that, you've spent more time with Gideon than I have.'

'True, and in all honesty, I don't think he has it in him. He's a little bit wet, and his head is full of ridiculous notions and schemes. He moves from one project to another; every week there's a different campaign to put his family back on the map. I think if Ambrose hadn't been killed, Gideon would have moved on to his next hare-brained obsession within a couple of weeks and forgotten all about it.'

'But if Ambrose brought it out into the open and Gideon wasn't allowed to forget it, then what?'

'Sophie, do be serious! How much attention do you think a ninety-year-old botany scandal is going to gather? It wasn't even worthy of being chip wrapper in the first place, let alone tomorrow's chip wrapper. He'd have received some joshing down the club, and then it would have been over. Ambrose, in the meantime, would have moved on to his next search for justice.

'No, Gideon isn't involved. Sorry, dear, you'll need to give this one further thought. What about that Fleur woman?'

Despite the barman saying it had been a man who'd tried to run Ambrose down, I was still giving her some consideration. The reckless driver might turn out to be unrelated to the murder.

'I'm trying to find some more contacts from her university days, but I can't find anyone else willing to talk to me. I'm going to have to contact Dr Fry again and see if he can convince anyone to speak to me.'

'And the police? You know, the ones paid to do this. Are you aware of how their investigation is going?'

'Don't pretend that you don't enjoy this as well! If you start lecturing me on leaving it to the professionals, then you'll fall firmly in the hypocrite category.'

'I am doing no such thing, but for all you know, they might have the killer in their sights, or even have arrested him or her, and be interrogating them while we speak.'

'I know, but if they haven't and I work it out first, well, I'll save them a job and valuable time and resources, while saving the

British taxpayer thousands of pounds.' I grinned. It was a daft argument, but it made me smile.

'And your plan now is to do what?'

'Head back to the Natural History Museum. I want to talk to Tess; I need to take Caleb a bit more seriously. He had a lot to lose, maybe everything.'

'Well, be careful. Mind you, that Caleb is rather good-looking. Play your cards right and he might ask you out.'

'That isn't worthy of a response, Joyce Brocklehurst.'

'Time is not on my side, my dear. I'm of the opinion that every opportunity should be considered and possibly grasped. In fact, just grasp; you can always reconsider later.'

She winked before turning to leave. Joyce had been the 'other woman' in the past, but she'd sworn off married men in recent years.

I looked around the café. There wasn't much left for me to do, so I put on an apron and got ready to start serving some customers. That way I'd feel less guilty when I took the afternoon off and went to the museum.

MARY ANNING, renowned fossil collector and one of the few women scientists in the first half of the 19th century, was showing a group of children an ammonite. As I walked past the group, the live interpreter playing Mary was pointing out the beautiful swirled shell trapped in the fossil. Her large seaweed-green coat and straw bonnet attracted the attention of curious tourists, so I watched them while waiting for Tess to join me.

She'd sounded a little nervous, but not unwilling to meet me, and I'd assured her that our conversation would be in complete confidence. I was running out of places to dig for information; I still had my suspicions about Fleur, who seemed so good at telling lies, I now trusted her about as far as I could throw her. But there were only so many questions I could ask, only so much

I could find out, and I had to accept the limitations of being someone who simply liked to stick her nose in rather than a police officer with lots of resources at my fingertips. If continuing to pursue Caleb brought me no joy, then I was going to be well and truly stuck. I was returning to Derbyshire tomorrow, and although I could probably continue to do some digging from there, leaving it to the police and getting on with my own life would probably be the sensible option. I hated to give up, though, and had never done so before.

Tess had an armful of files which landed on the café table with a thud.

'I seem to be spending the day doing nothing but taking minutes. I'm glad I have this break; it'll be nice to talk about something other than museum business, and not have to write it down, either.'

'Sit,' I insisted. 'I'll get you coffee and something packed with sugar, you look like you need it.' She smiled gratefully.

With a couple of Danish pastries before us, I got down to business. 'You might not be so keen on my alternative topic of conversation.'

'Don't worry, I know you want to talk about Caleb, or at least I assume you do. Once word got around that I was no longer involved with him, all sorts of people decided that they could tell me about all the other women he was involved with. I had no idea so many people knew about us; the rumour mill has been beavering away. I had my suspicions there were other women, but having it confirmed just means I want to kill him. So, what do you want to know?'

'Did you ever see Ambrose and Caleb arguing at all?'

'Occasionally, but that was always about work. Caleb would sometimes tell me what the issue was.'

'Was there anything that they argued about a lot?'

Tess licked sticky apricot jam off her fingers as she thought. 'They often disagreed about what Ambrose should be focusing on. He'd head off on his own little crusades, which was okay until it started impacting on his regular work for the department. They had a couple of big rows about that. I had to go and interrupt them on one occasion – you could hear them the length of the herbarium.' She stopped for a moment and looked at me intently. 'You must think I'm such an idiot.'

'Why would I think that?'

'Getting involved with a married man, and one with multiple women on the side. How could I not have worked it out, right? I was stupid to be so loyal to him, so naïve and blind.'

'I don't think that at all.'

'Well, I was an idiot because I let him treat me appallingly. Look at this.' She pulled out a brown folder from the pile on the table. A date was written on it in big black numbers: *11.06.21*. 'I've been typing up all the notes from a symposium that happened on this date. It was an evening thing and Caleb couldn't go to the presentation because he was taking his wife to the theatre to see a musical, but he was going to come back and join everyone for drinks later on. So, I had to make sure everything ran smoothly. I made endless notes and even wrote the report that he had to present on the proceedings, all the while knowing that he wasn't at the theatre with his wife at all; he was with one of his other women.'

'How do you know that for sure?'

'Because Michelle had told me weeks before that she was going out with her girlfriends to see the final performance of the musical. They were all staying in some fancy hotel and making a night of it. The photos were up on Facebook the next day.'

'And you're sure Caleb was with one of his other girlfriends?'

'Very sure. He put their romantic dinner and the taxi to and from the restaurant on his work credit card. He didn't care that I submit his credit card paperwork and gather the receipts, that I'd see it was a restaurant he'd taken me to, and that there was no work dinner scheduled in his diary. Of course, he charmed everyone on his return to the museum and commented on how good the musical had been. Luckily for him, no one asked him any specifics about the show.'

I looked at the date on the top of the file, recognising it. Not only was it Adam's birthday, it was also the date that the barman had said Ambrose was almost hit by a car driven recklessly by someone he recognised. I wondered what time Caleb had left the restaurant, and if this would put him outside The White Lion at around nine o'clock, but Tess said he'd been in a taxi. I asked Tess the name of the restaurant and she told me it was The Juniper, a place I was familiar with and a well-known romantic destination. Certainly not one you would pick for a business meal.

As Tess spoke, what looked like a mother – and one token father – and baby group started to get up. Baby buggies were moved around like a game of Tetris as everyone gathered their things and prepared to leave, making military manoeuvres look like, well, child's play. As they gradually moved away, I could see the tables beyond them, and at one a meeting was taking place. Amongst the attendees were Caleb and Molly, she sitting as far away from Caleb as it was possible for her to get. Next to her was a man in a very smart suit. I recognised him as a lawyer who had made a recent visit to Ravensbury House to see the Duke. There were a lot of smiles and, other than Molly, everyone looked quite relaxed; I assumed that things were going well and this was probably one of the final meetings before Caroline's paintings were handed over once the exhibition had closed.

A couple of people at the table started to reach for their jackets and put their paperwork away. I tuned back into Tess, who was still talking about gifts that had not been gratefully received, or not acknowledged at all. It seemed she had a long litany of complaints about Caleb that she was now happy to get out of her system, so I let her talk as my thoughts raced. I knew that Caleb's movements on the night of 11 June were important, I just couldn't work out why. If he'd been in a taxi, then he wasn't the man Ambrose had seen behind the wheel of the car, but it was niggling at me. It mattered.

I watched Caleb as he laughed at a comment from the lawyer, and then heard him call Molly's name across the table. Tess had felt her loyalty to the man had been stupid, naïve, and blind. It was then that everything fell into place. She wasn't the only one who had been blindly loyal to another.

I knew what had happened.

CHAPTER 40

'I can take you to see Zannah if you want? She's probably in the learning centre.'

Zannah had been asleep when I had returned from the Savoy last night. As I didn't have much time left with her before I returned to Derbyshire, I would take every chance to see my friend that I could get. As sure as I was, I didn't want to act on what I had worked out until I had talked it through with Joyce and Mark, on the off chance they thought I had lost my mind, so waiting an hour wasn't going to be a problem. I didn't believe that anyone else was at risk from Ambrose's killer.

'It'll take forever to go through the museum, we'll have to fight through the crowds. I'll take you downstairs and we can cut through the basement.'

Using the pass that hung on a lanyard around her neck, Tess accessed a locked door marked private and led the way down some stairs that opened out into a large basement with paths marked out on the floor in yellow tape. We wound our way past shelves stacked high with boxes. A forklift truck sat in a corner, and all sorts of doors led to worlds of – I assumed – scientific discovery: jars full of specimens with bug eyes and long scaly tails. Imagining eccentric scientists with long grey beards and round metal spectacles perched on the end of their noses, I peered through the glass panel in a door and was greeted by the mundane sight of hundreds of computer screens and keyboards, all looking rather old and dust-covered. A box full of computer mice was the closest thing to zoological specimens.

We rounded a corner and I was met by the sight of a giraffe standing guard at a point where the yellow marked path formed a crossroads. Next to him – I decided it was a he – stood an elephant. This is what I had expected. I stopped and looked at them, and they looked back.

Both Tess and I turned at the sound of voices. In the distance, past a long line of shelves full of antlers, I could see Caleb, Molly and a couple of others from their meeting.

'Where are they going? The herbarium is upstairs.'

'The picture store is down there. He's probably showing them more of the collection. It's vast, you'd think we were the National Gallery.'

'What's through there?' I pointed to a door without any glass windows. Someone had attached a handwritten sign that said, '*Do Not Feed the Animals*'.

'Just more old collections.'

'Tess? Is that you, Tess?' A rather hesitant male voice called down past an antelope and a wolf.

'It's me, Gerry. Hang on. Sophie, I won't be a minute. Just wait here. Gerry's been trying to get hold of me for a while, but his office is down here and I always forget about him. I really ought to see what he needs.'

'Sure, I'll just chat to this lot.'

However, the giraffe wasn't very forthcoming and the elephant seemed to be preoccupied by something over my shoulder. Once I'd also been snubbed by a kangaroo, my attention was drawn back to the chatter of Caleb's group, who were still in the basement. I wanted to be absolutely certain of something that Tess had told me, so I walked around the corner to where Caleb was opening a pair of large cabinet doors and pulling out a metal shelf on rollers.

I tapped Molly on the shoulder. 'Do you have a minute?'

'Sure,' she whispered. 'There's only so long I can pretend to be interested in what Caleb says these days.'

'This is a bit delicate, but I need to ask you about an evening you might have spent with Caleb. Did you go to the Juniper Restaurant with him last month? It was a Friday, and he was meant to be at a conference that evening.'

Her eyes searched my face and I couldn't read the expression that she held me with.

'Can I ask why?'

'I wanted to check his whereabouts at a particular time.'

That seemed to make her relax a little, but just a little.

'Yes, I was.'

'Do you recall what time you left?'

'Why does it matter?'

'There was an incident with Ambrose and a car that evening. I was hoping you could remember.' I smiled reassuringly. She scanned my face again and I tried to shape my expression into one of support.

'I'm not sure. Around nine, I think.'

'Did he leave in a taxi?'

'Yes.'

'Thanks, Molly. I know you probably don't want to talk about your relationship with him any more than you need to, so I'm sorry I had to bring it up again.'

She looked over her shoulder. Caleb was closing up the cabinet.

'I should go.'

'Of course. Just think, this will hopefully be one of the last times you have to sit through a meeting with him.'

She nodded. 'Thank goodness, I'll be so pleased when it's over.'

I watched her return to the group, and then made my way back to the giraffe.

Tess had yet to return and my attention was drawn back to the door with the handwritten sign. I gave a gentle tug on the handle and the door opened easily. A series of grubby windows high up the full length of one wall threw a milky light onto the shelves. The syrupy glow came and went as the public walked past, the windows revealing only their feet and ankles, and I remembered I was below ground level.

In the darkened room, tall industrial metal shelving housed a vast array of creatures, most of them stuffed and attached to wooden plinths. It looked as though a multitude of hunting lodges and Victorian smoking rooms had been emptied of their owners' prize displays. Tatty cardboard boxes had numbers written on them, which no doubt meant something to someone. I tried not to look in the animals' eyes; when I did, I felt either fear or heart-wrenching pity. I understood how much we had been able to learn from collections such as these, but it was also a reminder of how our Victorian ancestors had travelled the world, laying claim to anything and everything in their path. This general sense of arrogance was one that the human race had maintained to this day.

I was deep in thought when I saw a shadow move in a way that was different from those caused by the stream of pedestrian traffic outside the window. I heard the chime of metal on metal behind me, followed by a creak and the sound of wood being dragged on a hard surface. I sensed something over my shoulder, or above my head. I wasn't sure which.

Spinning round, I glanced up as a panther loomed down at me from the top shelf. With one leap, it made a bid for freedom, flinging itself into the air and descending at great speed towards me. I threw myself out of the way, but one outstretched paw caught my shoulder and I felt the claws drag the length of my upper arm.

I grabbed my arm and turned. The cat lay motionless on its side, frozen mid pounce. It was hard to tell in the shadows, but I didn't think it had drawn blood.

I heard the clang of metal on metal again as a long grey shelf support loomed into my sight line. It caught the side of another shelf briefly, and then came straight for me, chopping down from above towards my head. I ducked behind a metal filing cabinet, which caught the weight of the blow, feeling the impact vibrate through the drawer I was leaning against. Then I gathered enough sense to run to the far end of the row.

Everything was grey and black; every other colour in the room had been sucked from its host by the dust and shadows. Until now I'd been too surprised to feel fear, but as I stood at the end of the shelves, trying to decide which way to run, I realised my heart was beating so hard it was at risk of bursting out of my chest. I had no idea which way to go; I had lost all sense of direction.

'Who's there?' I called out. 'Who is it?' Had someone actually known I was here? Had they accidentally knocked the cat off the shelf, or was it a deliberate act?

No response. Their silence was even more frightening than if they had spoken. I wanted to know something about them, get a sense of where they were in the room, who they were, what they wanted. I refused to accept just how terrified I was. Right now, I needed to hide, or get out. Right now, I needed to avoid that long, narrow piece of metal which someone wanted to use to split my head open. Right now, I needed to take a chance and run one way or the other, so I ran in the direction that I felt would most likely lead me to the door.

I'd made the wrong choice.

Standing at the far end of the next row, side on to me and grasping the metal bar like an oversized sword which she was struggling to control, was Molly Flinders.

CHAPTER 41

Molly turned and saw me a millisecond after I had laid eyes on her. We both jumped, neither of us expecting the other.

'MOLLY, WHAT THE HELL ARE YOU DOING?' I screamed. She turned, raising the bar a little higher. It looked unwieldy and swayed slightly.

'MOLLY?' I realised with some relief that the likelihood of her having a dead accurate aim with that thing was limited, but if it did hit its target, it would do a lot of damage. All I needed to do was stay out of her way and hope she didn't find a better object to use, or attempt to attack me with her hands. I wasn't the strongest of people and my response would probably be a high-pitched scream while flailing my arms around with my eyes shut, hoping for the best, which had been my approach as a child in the school playground. It had worked back then, but mainly because the other children stepped back in order to watch my lunatic impression of a whirling dervish. The outcome was likely to be a little different this time.

'Sophie, are you in here?' I heard the door brush against the floor. 'Sophie?'

'Tess, stay out!' I shouted. 'Get help!'

'What's happened? Are you okay?'

Molly had turned towards the sound of Tess's voice. Her silence was creeping me out.

'GET OUT AND GET HELP!' I shouted as loud as I could.

'What's going on?'

I'd never been more pleased to hear Caleb's voice. Molly still held the metal bar, but her confidence seemed to waver and I watched her shoulders sag. She looked defeated.

'You should have just left it alone, Sophie. No one would have found out, no one was questioning it. Everyone – the police and you were all looking in the wrong direction.' When Molly finally broke her vow of silence, she sounded as defeated as she looked.

'What are you talking about, Mol?' Caleb asked, desperation and confusion in his voice. I was the one to answer.

'It's quite simple, really, isn't it, Molly? Your speeding ticket wasn't really yours.' I turned to Caleb. 'Molly wasn't driving Oliver's car when it was caught by a speeding camera, it was Oliver himself. I'm going to guess that he already has a lot of points on his licence, and having it suspended would have been great newspaper fodder *and* given his father something else to hold against him. So he asked one of the family's most loyal members of staff to say she was driving the car. It wasn't a big deal, no one need find out. After all, Molly often did drive his car.

'Only Ambrose found out, because it was Oliver who nearly hit him that night. I guess the Duke must have said something to Ambrose or he overheard Molly and the Duke talking about the speeding ticket – you said yourself, Molly, that the Duke had been teasing you about it. Ambrose put two and two together, and always wanted justice to be done, whatever the issue. The problem is that the paperwork had already been signed and sent, and if Ambrose told anyone what had really happened, the penalty you and Oliver both faced was a prison sentence.

'You tried to convince Ambrose to stay quiet, didn't you,

Molly? But when Ambrose said he wanted to meet with the Duke, you guessed what it must be about, even though Ambrose wouldn't tell you. You knew there was a risk he was going to drop you in it. You couldn't go to prison; you had to shut Ambrose up.'

I looked back at Caleb, who was staring at Molly with an expression of horror on his face.

'You, Molly, were working late the night the Duke brought his guests, including Ambrose, back to Ravensbury House, but you left before Ambrose, put the hoodie on, and then waited for him.' I wondered if she would contradict me. She remained silent. 'You'd grabbed a letter opener just in case, and when he remained determined to go ahead and tell the truth to the Duke, you stabbed him in the alleyway. I bet you were terrified when he walked away like nothing had happened; he really didn't know you'd stabbed him. I assume either the shock of seeing what must have appeared to be a dead man walking or the fear you'd be identified by at least one of the many cameras en route stopped you from following. Instead, you discarded your weapon and hoodie and went home. You must have been so relieved when you heard the next day that he had in fact died.'

Caleb had stepped forward. I could see his face between the legs and tails of various stuffed animals on a shelf. Then we all started as the room was plunged into blinding light. I blinked a few times. When my vision adjusted, I could see Molly was doing the same thing, but could also focus enough to keep Caleb at bay with the metal bar.

'Molly, don't you think you should put that down?' Detective Sergeant Knapp had a remarkably calm and gentle voice. 'I'm going to ask everyone else to leave. Okay?'

Caleb walked slowly out of the room.

'Sophie, go round the other way. Molly isn't going to stop you.'

I looked at Molly. It was only at that moment when I was hit by the crushing blow that I had lost someone I really liked. Molly had become my friend as well as my colleague. I didn't feel angry, just incredibly sad.

CHAPTER 42

I sat on a concrete fire-escape step with a bottle of water that Zannah had grabbed for me from the café. The view before me was of the staff car park and loading bay, surrounded on three sides by the grubby stone walls of the museum that were hidden from public view. The police had asked me to stay on site as they hadn't finished with me, but I wanted fresh air. Not that it was very fresh; we were only a couple of feet from a shelter that had been built for the smokers amongst the museum staff.

'When did you work out that it was Molly?' Zannah asked, as wide-eyed as she had been when she first came to find me after I'd sent her a message.

'After I decided to simplify things. I spend my working life surrounded by history, so my instinct was to follow any trail that led to something that had happened in the past, even the distant past. I had been seeking skeletons in people's closets, but it wasn't that complicated. The comment from The White Lion barman about Ambrose knowing the person who had tried to run him over – or who I assumed had tried to run him over – got me thinking about recent events. I decided it had to be connected. It was too much of a coincidence.

'Until then, I had been thinking about Fleur, Caleb or Gideon as the possible killers, but the driver being male ruled out Fleur. Gideon can't drive, so he was out of the equation. Then there was the date on the police paperwork in Molly's office. I clocked it as it matched the evening Ambrose was almost hit, which also happened to be the night of my ex Adam's birthday when a friend of mine saw a drunk Oliver leaving the restaurant she and Adam work at. She said that Oliver was usually sent home in a taxi when he was the worse for wear, and even though she couldn't remember who had called a taxi for him that night, we both assumed someone must have.

'Because Ambrose had told the barman that it was a male driver, I didn't initially think that it could have anything to do with Molly. But I knew someone was lying. If I could find out who had been in that car, then I could probably piece together the rest. Maybe not definitively, but at least I'd know where I had to dig a bit deeper.

'Caleb was a very strong contender, but when Tess told me that he'd been at a restaurant around the time the near miss happened and had travelled there and home in a taxi, I knew it couldn't be him. Even if Ambrose had been mistaken about the gender of the driver, the fact that Caleb had been with Molly ruled her out, too. But it could have been Oliver.

'I started to wonder if he had actually driven home from the restaurant over the limit, and had nearly hit Ambrose not because he meant him any harm, but because he was too drunk to be driving. That led me on to driving offences. It was Molly who said she had been caught speeding that night when actually she had been having dinner with Caleb. It wasn't adding up. When I was with Tess earlier, she commented that she had been blindly and naively loyal to Caleb, which reminded me that much the same had been said about Molly in relation to Oliver. She had covered for him in the past, helped him out when others wouldn't have had the patience, and it all started to fall into place.

'She had not been behind the wheel of Oliver's car that night, but she did make it home from the restaurant in time to be in when he arrived at her flat and asked for her help. He may not have seen the red traffic light, or the fact he'd almost mowed Ambrose down, but the flash of a speed camera is designed to catch the eye, so I'm guessing he saw that alright. He couldn't afford any more points on his licence, and Molly knew that.

'What she didn't know when she agreed to take the points on her own licence, was that a principled man who was renowned for wanting to see justice done knew full well that it had been Oliver driving that night. And if Ambrose told the police what she had done, which he was highly likely to do, she faced a prison sentence. To avoid that, she clearly decided, would be worth killing for.'

'Can you really go to prison for taking a speeding fine on someone else's behalf?'

'Oh yes, there have been a number of cases in the press recently about politicians who have done the exact same thing. They all went to prison, and just as they experienced, there would be a lot of press attention on Oliver if the same happened to him.'

'Incredible, Soph. I don't know how you do it.'

'Mark said I tend to look at the bigger picture, the relationships between people. It was the relationship between Molly and the Fitzwilliam-Scott family that was key.'

I finished talking and realised I was exhausted. The adrenalin rush that I had been riding since Molly had tried to attack me had come to the end.

'How are you feeling now, Sophie?' DS Knapp looked genuinely concerned. He'd been sitting quietly on a step below and listening to our conversation, but now he turned to face me.

'Fine, thank you.'

'I'm beginning to suspect this is something you make a habit of.'

I decided it would be best if I didn't say anything in response.

'Was she right, though, sergeant?' asked Zannah. 'Molly claimed she'd been driving the car when it was actually Oliver, and Ambrose found out so she killed him?'

'Yes.'

'So, she's admitted it?'

He nodded. 'I phoned the traffic division. The car was seen in the area near Molly's flat on the night of the offence, which helped support her claim that she'd been driving it. I imagine that Oliver Fitzwilliam-Scott realised he had been caught on camera speeding, drove to Molly's in a bit of a panic and managed to convince her to take the blame. He then left the car with her and found another way to get home. If they hadn't been rumbled, then Molly would have had three points on her otherwise spotless licence and Oliver wouldn't have been suspected of anything.

'However, Ambrose found out and threatened to tell the Duke, and then the police. The same loyalty that convinced Molly to cover up for Oliver's speeding also drove her to kill Ambrose to protect them both from an even worse penalty. We did check Molly out as part of our enquiries, but other than those newly gained points, she has a faultless record and an excellent reputation with her employers. There was absolutely nothing about her that could have made her a suspect.

'We at the Met owe you a thank you, Sophie. DI Grey will probably give you the reprimand that you also deserve, but I do think you should get some thanks. But if you do make a habit of being an amateur sleuth, please could you limit your activities to Derbyshire?' He raised his eyebrows at me as he started to get up, but his wagging finger was accompanied by a smile that I could only describe as cheeky.

Without thinking, I grabbed his arm to prevent him standing. 'One thing?'

'Yes?'

'Do you think Oliver knew Molly had killed Ambrose?'

'Molly says not. I imagine we can charge him with perverting the course of justice, and he'll go to prison for that, but I doubt we can prove he knew about the murder.'

'He's rather cute,' commented Zannah as we watched DS Knapp walk away. 'Works out too, by the looks of things.'

'I'm sure he left a business card back at the house. I could get his number for you, and you could ask him out.'

'No, I couldn't.' But the look on her face told me that she could, and most likely would. 'Talking of men, how are things with Adam?'

'There isn't any*thing* with Adam, we're not even friends. I'm sorry he got involved with Oliver's "money for meetings" scam; I rather hoped that he would come out of prison a reformed man, but clearly not. Oh God!' I groaned. 'The Duke and Duchess, this will devastate them. I don't think they could give two hoots what the press say, but their son will almost certainly be facing a prison sentence.'

CHAPTER 43

London stretched out before me, set against the backdrop of a clear blue sky. I looked out over a city that had remained unchanged for hundreds of years while simultaneously adapting to the fast-paced, ambitious new centuries, my eye drawn, as it always was, to St Paul's Cathedral. The 300-year-old masterpiece that had been born from the flames of the Great Fire of London had witnessed world wars, hosted weddings and funerals of the great and the good, and was one of my favourite buildings.

The Thames snaked its way under bridges and past landmarks. No longer clogged with cargo ships packed so closely together that you could walk from one bank to the other, it now carried tourists and police boats. The Tower of London protected the Crown Jewels from the encroaching office blocks that looked set to overpower the Yeoman Warders and storm the gates at any moment.

As our London Eye pod slowly lifted us heavenwards, I took in the city that I had called home for many years. I would never regret leaving and moving to Derbyshire, but it was a classic case of *absence makes the heart grow fonder.*

Joyce, Mark, Zannah and I had booked an early morning ride on the London Eye before we all went our separate ways. Mark was returning to Charleton House that afternoon as he had a number of VIP tours to deliver over the weekend. Joyce was moving into a hotel and spending the weekend shopping before returning home on Sunday night, and I had decided to stay a couple more days with Zannah and was determined to do as many touristy things as possible.

'Madame Tussauds?' Joyce said with disdain. 'Why would you waste your money at such a tacky, tourist-riddled venue?'

'Because it's silly and fun and I haven't been since I was twelve.'

'Come on, Joyce, we all know it's where you go to get makeup tips.' Mark grinned at her. We weren't alone in the pod so he knew she couldn't respond with violence. Instead, she glared at him before turning to focus on the view ahead of her. Today, she'd opted for a silk blouse covered in puffy white clouds against a pale blue background, so it was hard to tell where Joyce ended and the view began.

'How have the Duke and Duchess taken the news?' asked Zannah. 'You told me they were very fond of Molly.'

I sighed. 'They are. I haven't seen them, they weren't at the house when I went to collect some things last night. Mark?'

Mark stepped over to join us and rested his back against the hand rail. He folded his arms.

'The Duke didn't say much when I saw him. I think he's still processing what Oliver was up to: taking money from people in return for introducing them to him, manipulating him and trying to benefit financially from his reputation and contacts. I know he'll be deeply hurt by that. Of course, the worse thing is the prison sentence Oliver is now facing. I spoke to Joe last night – he was round at ours having a beer with Bill. He said it was unlikely that the family lawyers will be able to help him avoid that, it's all very cut and dried. I'm just grateful Oliver's not the next in line. Can you imagine him as the Duke of Ravensbury?'

Joyce swivelled her head around with such force, I was afraid she'd strain herself. 'Dear God, that doesn't bear thinking about. I'd much rather have dead bodies popping up all over the place than have him running the house.' Her rather loud declaration caused the heads of the other tourists in the pod to swivel. A mother grabbed her young son and pushed him to the far side, away from us.

'Annabelle was particularly furious about Molly,' Mark continued. 'I really think that if she got her hands on her, we'd have a second body to deal with. They got on really well, or so Annabelle thought. She's also mad on her parents' behalf, they put so much trust in Molly. Her brother, on the other hand... well, I don't think Annabelle's the least bit surprised that he's got himself into this level of trouble.'

Mark turned back to the view. He had been uncharacteristically quiet when he'd first heard the news about Molly, and until this morning had barely spoken. I knew he held a lot of affection for the family, and the outcome of Ambrose's murder had come as a shock to him, too.

'Sophie,' Joyce said as she sidled up to me awkwardly, 'can I have a word?'

'Sure, what's up?'

'I owe you an apology.'

I stared at her, unable to move. I had no idea how to react to a sentence that seemed so strange coming out of her mouth.

'When I drew up the list of people who had access to the letter openers, I said everyone who had been gifted one by me had been accounted for. Well, I didn't actually check if the Duchess still had hers. I'd shown her the first one that had been made using the final design months ago and she'd kept it. I guess she brought it to London with her and put it in her office at the house. It just seemed so ludicrous to me that her name should be associated with the investigation in any way, I discounted that one. I forgot that although we don't have regular access to their apartments in the house, a number of people do, including Molly. I presume she just picked it up off the Duchess's desk.'

I nodded. 'Don't worry about it. Like you say, any number of people could have had access to that particular opener. Even if the Duchess's had been confirmed as the murder weapon, it wouldn't have helped narrow things down.'

'That's good, then.' She sounded immediately like her old self, and I chortled at how easily she had recovered her poise and confidence. Any sense of mortification was short-lived.

Mark returned his attention to us. 'So, what about the Earl of Baxworth, does he feature in your future?' he asked Joyce. 'Do you think you can help reinstate his family's good name and bank balance, and return him to "society"?'

'Not likely. I haven't heard from the wet lump since we all ambushed him the other night. I understand his indignation, a little, but he should grow a…' she glanced at the family, who were cowering even further into the far side of the pod '…he should toughen up. I could never be involved with a man like that. I want a sparring partner, not a little poodle who needs patting on the head and telling his latest hare-brained scheme has legs or crackpot idea is a solid piece of historical fact. Shakespeare? For heaven's sake, his family can't even write a valid cheque, let alone be the true authors of the Bard's work. Bonkers, the lot of them.'

After a pause, she asked, 'Do you think anyone has ever fallen out of one of these?'

'You'd need a tin opener,' Mark replied.

'Right, everyone, photo time.' Joyce handed her phone to a startled woman among the people sharing our pod. 'Gather round. Are you ready, dear? You do know how to work these things, don't you?'

The poor woman looked a little put out and made it clear she did indeed know what she was doing. Joyce grabbed Mark and pulled him in a little closer.

'You need to straighten your moustache. It's dropping a little on the right.' Mark sighed and gave it a twist. 'Not that right, my right… up a little… oh, for heaven's sake.' She reached across his face and attempted to curl one end. 'Eugh, all that horrid oil.' She wiped her fingers on Mark's shoulder. 'Right, everyone,' she trilled, 'all together now, smile at the camera and say, "Murder".'

I HOPE YOU ENJOYED THIS BOOK

I really hope you enjoyed reading this book as much as I did writing it. I would love you more than I love coffee, gin and chocolate brownies if you could go on to Amazon and leave a review right this very moment. Even if it's just a one sentence comment, your words make a massive difference.

Amazon reviews are a huge boost to independently published authors like me who don't have big publishing houses to spread the word for us. The more reviews, the more likely it is that this book will be discovered by other readers.

Thank you so much.

READ A FREE CHARLETON HOUSE MYSTERY

Building a relationship with my readers is one of the best things about writing. I occasionally send newsletters with details on new releases, special offers, interviews and articles relating to The Charleton House Mysteries.

Sign up to my mailing list and you'll also receive the very first Charleton House Mystery, *A Stately Murder*.

Head to my website for your free copy and find out what happens when Sophie stumbles across the victim of the first murder Charleton House has ever known.

www.katepadams.com

ABOUT THE AUTHOR

After 25 years working in some of England's finest buildings, Kate P. Adams has turned to murder.

Kate grew up in Derbyshire, the setting for the Charleton House Mysteries, and went on to work in theatres around the country, the Natural History Museum - London, the University of Oxford and Hampton Court Palace. Every day she explored darkened corridors and rooms full of history behind doors the public never get to enter. Kate spent years in these beautiful buildings listening to fantastic tales, wondering where the bodies were hidden, and hoping that she'd run into a ghost or two.

Kate has an unhealthy obsession with finding the perfect cup of coffee, enjoys a gin and tonic, and is managed by Pumpkin, a domineering tabby cat who is a little on the large side. Now that she lives in the USA, writing the Charleton House Mysteries allows Kate to go home to be her beloved Derbyshire everyday, in her head at least.

www.katepadams.com

ACKNOWLEDGEMENTS

Thank you to my beta readers Joanna Hancox, Lynne McCormack, Helen McNally, Eileen Minchin and Rosanna Summers. Your honesty and insightful comments help make my books so much better than they would otherwise be.

Many thanks to my advance readers; your support and feedback means a great deal to me.

Thank you to Dawn Sanders for her insight into the world of botany. Anne Griffin ensured my memories of the Natural History Museum remained fresh and made me laugh as we reminisced about our various escapades behind the scenes at the Natural History Museum, London. Frances Sampayo introduced me to the wonderful Chelsea Physic Garden and gave me a lot more fascinating information than made it to the final edit.

I'm extremely grateful to Richard Mason, my police advisor who guides me on procedure and makes sure I am, largely, within the law. When I break the rules, that's all me!

My talented editor Alison Jack, and Julia Gibbs, my eagle-eyed proofreader. It is an education and a pleasure to work with them.

Thank you to my wife Sue, who has yet to balk at the amount of time I spend with murder on my mind.

Printed in Great Britain
by Amazon